Sand Dollar COVE

Sand Dollar COVE

NANCY NAIGLE

Crossroads Publishing House

www.CrossroadsPublishingHouse.com

Sand Dollar Cove
Copyright © 2015, Nancy Naigle
Trade Paperback ISBN: 978-0991127269

Release, April 2015

Crossroads Publishing House
P.O. Box 55
Pfafftown, NC 27040

To all my beach loving friends.

Chapter One

As soon as Elli Eversol pushed her toes into the gritty sand on the beach, wonderful memories swept away the stress she'd carried on the five-hour drive from Charlotte. Temperatures were already hovering in the sixties, unseasonably warm for March on the North Carolina coast, especially for this early in the morning. With her shoes and socks in hand, she walked down to the pier, her footsteps leaving clear imprints in the crusted top layer of sand.

Filling her lungs with ocean air, the only thing missing from her memories of the beach was the scent of suntan lotion, but summer was just a few months away.

Sand Dollar Cove still held a special place in her heart. Every summer for as long as she could remember, she'd stayed here with Nana and Pops at their beach house. The Sol~Mate had been her home away from home on summer breaks until she'd gone away to college. Her plan had been to move here once she graduated, but Dad had made her promise that she'd work in a city for two years before making a decision to settle in Sand Dollar

Cove. He'd grown up here and, according to Nana and Pops, Daddy couldn't wait to get out of the small beach town. She'd never understood it, but he must've been onto something: Even though she'd moved to Charlotte with the plan to get some experience under her belt just to make him happy, she'd been there ever since. Two years turned into five, and she stayed so busy she hadn't even had the time to think about moving since.

Waves crashed against the pier, filling the air with a misty spray. The seagulls above seemed to laugh at some inside joke between them. At least at this time of the year the sand was cool. In the summer there were days you were forced to use your towel and shirt as stepping stones to get back to the parking lot or else burn your feet. After a winter of closed-toe shoes, it sure felt good to walk the beach again.

A young couple stood under the pier. The water lapped at their ankles as the guy leaned in, probably promising her the world. She'd been that girl once. The crash of the waves dulling her sensibilities and drowning out her voice of reason. It was a long time ago, but her chest ached at the memory of the heartbreak of that summer.

Elli silently wished the girl under the pier better luck than she'd had. Between those broken promises and then losing Pops just a few weeks later, that summer had been the worst of her life. Maybe work wasn't the only reason her trips back to Sand Dollar Cove had become more infrequent over the years. Maybe these memories had a little to do with it too.

As she got closer to the pier, the No Trespassing signs and yellow caution tape caught her off-guard. The insurance company probably demanded they mark it to keep from being held liable, should someone try to fish before the repairs were complete. But still, it was unsettling.

The recent nor'easter had done even more damage to the pier, sweeping a huge gap right out of the center of the remaining pilings. Seeing it for the first time in person, it was a lot worse than she'd realized. The pier looked like a snaggle-toothed jack-o'-lantern about two weeks after Halloween. A swirl of concern swept through her. If the town didn't get busy on repairs they could miss one of the biggest moneymakers of the summer tourist season, Memorial Day weekend.

Her bright mood faded. Pops had built those shops on the pier nearly fifty years ago. When the hurricane damaged them, Elli had started an online fundraiser to repair them. The Buy A Board campaign had been more successful than she'd ever dreamed; the donations more than doubling her initial goal in only a few weeks. For a $250 donation, donors could opt to have their names displayed on one of the boards used to make the repairs. That had been the most popular option, and the smaller donations had added up quickly too.

When Nana mentioned that she hadn't been able to renew her license for the shops, Elli had assumed Nana just hadn't gotten around to it. Now she wondered if perhaps the town was stalling on issuing them because they'd fallen behind on this project. *Fallen behind* was being kind. It looked like no one had done a thing.

She glanced at her watch. Right now she was due at the Carolina By The Sea Resort and Spa. Breaking into a jog, she got back to her car and used her socks to swat the damp sand off her feet, then put her shoes back on.

It was a short ride to the spa from here. Elli pulled her car into the last parking spot at the far end of the resort near the restaurant.

March could be desolate, and many of the businesses chose to shut down completely until Memorial Day. But Pam seemed to be doing a big business, if the parking lot was any indication.

Inside, the place was bustling. Filled nearly to capacity in the shoulder seasons, pre- and post-summer, was a big deal in a small beach town such as this.

"You made good time," Pam said, rushing to Elli and pulling her into a big hug.

"It's so good to see you." Elli pulled back from the hug. She still thought of Pam as her teenaged beach buddy. Practically twins, except Pam had dark hair and brown eyes, so whenever they got together and Pam was pulled together, all business, it always took her by surprise. "You look great."

Pam struck a pose. "Spa living suits me."

"Apparently. I could hardly sleep last night knowing I'd be seeing you today."

"Some things never change. Welcome back." Pam motioned her to follow. "You should have just driven down last night."

They settled in a corner booth, and a waiter dropped off menus and took their drink orders. "True, but I'd promised Bob I'd take care of some things before I left town. We've got a big open house today. So I did all the prep for that last night."

"Y'all staying busy?"

"Very busy," Elli said. "Bob and I are a good team. We have different specialties, so between us we have a steady workload no matter what the economy is doing. That's a blessing in the real estate market right now."

"And there's still nothing between you two? I swear if I had a Realtor as good-looking as he is, I might never settle on a house to buy. I'd just look and look and look."

"He is cute, but no. He's *so* not my type. Nothing but business between the two of us." Elli thanked the waiter for her cup of tea and glanced over the menu as she spoke. "And frankly, that's good for business. Besides, now that I know him so well I can see that I'd never be his type either. He likes those high-maintenance girls who stroke his ego day and night. Not exactly my style if you know what I mean."

"I know the type. But hey, as long as he's selling houses it's all good, right?"

"My thoughts exactly."

"Every once in a while a customer will talk about buying a place here. Are you still licensed to sell here in the cove?"

Elli took a sip of her tea. "Sure am. I've kept that up to date. Never know when it'll come in handy."

"Next time someone goes all gaga for Sand Dollar Cove, I'll give them your name."

"That would be great. It would give me a reason to come more often too." She closed the menu and set it aside. "I've got to be better about that. Nana is not getting any younger, and I feel so awful for letting so much time slip by between visits. I don't know how I let that happen."

"Well, you're here now."

"It was good timing. That pier is looking right pitiful."

"Yeah. It's not good. I'm so glad you were able to raise money to help fix the shops," Pam said. "They're part of the tradition around here."

"One quick mention on social media that I needed someone good with a router to help engrave the planks in exchange for room and board here, I had no less than half a dozen responses."

"I'm not surprised. I'm using social media for a big part of my marketing campaign for the resort, and it's paying off big time."

"I thought I'd end up with someone local, but the guy who is coming is from California. He'll be here this week to start personalizing the boards in exchange for room and board at Sol~Mate."

"Your grandmother will be in seventh heaven with someone to dote on."

"Nana loves fussing over people."

Pam nodded. "You know she's been canceling some of her hair appointments. I'm not complaining, but it's not like her. It's probably good that you're here to check in on her."

"That really isn't like her. Thanks for mentioning that." As if she didn't already feel guilty for being away so long, if something were wrong with Nana, she'd never forgive herself. "That worries me."

"She seems fine when she comes. Maybe she's just slowing down," Pam said. "How old is she?"

"Seventy-five. It's hard to believe though. She's so active I never think of her as getting old." She had to do a better job of making the time in her schedule to come visit.

"We're all getting older."

"Yeah, so let's quit talking about age. That's just depressing."

"Women fighting the battle against aging keep my spa full. I'm not ever going to complain about getting older."

Joy filled Elli's heart at her friend's success. No college. Just great business sense. The girl could make anything work. "Good point. I'm thinking that the beach and pedicures is a real money-making racket too. One quick walk on the beach on my way here and I pretty much ruined mine."

"Well, you and Nana should come Monday. My treat."

"That'll be great. We'll take you up on that if Nana doesn't have plans."

"Good." Pam pulled out her phone, and her fingers swept across the screen "All set. Gosh, Elli, it's really good to see you. I've really missed you. I'd been counting the days to your visit next month. It's such a treat to have you here sooner. I was surprised when I got your text."

"Brody, my California volunteer, said he had to be out on this coast for something else, and if I'd move up the date he'd cover his own travel. So instead of next month, he's coming this week."

"Perfect."

"Exactly. Now I can use that money for some other upgrade. That Buy A Board campaign was an awesome idea. We'll be able to get those shops in shipshape. Thank you so much for coming up with that idea. Your ideas always come through." The waiter filled Elli's cup with tea. "Thank you." Pam lifted her glass to Elli's, and they giggled as though they were sixteen again.

High school. That was when Elli met Pam, over summer break while Elli was staying with her grandparents at Sol~Mate. They hit it off and looked forward to every summer break and family visit after that.

When Elli had taken up her grandparents' offer to use part of their shop on the pier to start a summer business, it was Pam who'd helped Elli put the plan to paper for her homemade ice pop business. She'd made enough money that first summer to pay for her books and classes for two semesters. Her parents had been so pleased that they'd matched her penny for penny. It had made it a no-brainer to focus just on studies, then take each summer off to replenish her funds. Besides, she'd always loved this town, and hanging out on the beach in the sun was good work if you could get it. Working here was like play.

Elli said, "I was thinking maybe I could take you and Jack down to Nags Head to get those crab cakes we love. Think he could get an afternoon off while I'm in town?"

"About that." Pam took a long swig of her mimosa. Her expression stilled and grew serious.

Elli sat back. "What? You're giving me a bad vibe."

"We're separated."

"You're what?" Elli put her teacup down. "What happened? Y'all were perfect together. Are you kidding me?"

"Not kidding."

Elli's throat tightened. "What did he do? Are you okay?"

"Nothing. Relax. We just started moving in different directions."

"When did this happen?" She felt suddenly very left out. "Doesn't the maid of honor have some kind of right to be in the loop on this kind of stuff?"

"It's not that big of a deal. Things here at the spa are finally really taking off. His career is too. Only that meant a promotion that would relocate him to Texas. I didn't want to hold him back, and he didn't want to ask me to give up the spa. Besides, closing Carolina By The Sea would be very bad for this town. You know we don't have that many businesses here to start with. It's my hometown. I want to do my part, and I don't want to live anywhere else. Really it's for the best."

"And it's amicable?"

"Completely. That's why it seemed so weird to call and say, 'Hey, Elli, guess what, I'm getting a divorce.' There wasn't anything anybody you or anyone else could do."

"You're not sad at all?"

She shrugged. "Not really. Things were good, but they were mostly comfortable. It's for the best."

"If you say so." Sadness swept over Elli. For some reason Jack and Pam not making it felt like less hope for her to find a lasting relationship.

CHAPTER TWO

Elli drove from the resort straight to her grandmother's beach house. Sol~Mate had been Elli's home away from home nearly every summer of her life. Nothing ever changed, and she loved that about this place.

The tall sea oats waved a welcome back hello as she took the private beach road. She stopped at the mailbox, which was filled to the gills. Juggling the stack, she plopped all of it in the passenger seat and drove to the house. She parked alongside Nana's minivan, stacked all the mail and tucked it into the top of her overnight bag to make it easier to carry.

Like most beach houses around here, the front door was on the second level. She balanced her load and held her hand slightly above the wooden rail as she hiked up the steep stairs. Over the years she'd had more than her fair share of splinters from the old hand rail, and those were never fun.

She opened the screen door, rapped twice on the front door, and walked on in.

"Nana?" The smell of something sweet wafted through the front room. "It's me, Nana. Elli."

Sandy Eversol walked into the living room with a kitchen towel slung over her shoulder, wiping her hands on her apron. Elli loved the way Nana's eyes lit up when she saw her. If she was ever feeling down, that look would lift her out of it in a snap.

"Why didn't you tell me you were coming?" She threw her arms open, and Elli walked right into them.

"Surprise."

"A good one. What are you doing in town? I thought you weren't coming until next month."

"I had the chance to expedite the plan, so I jumped on it. Besides, it's been too long since I've seen you in person. On the phone is just not the same." Nana seemed like her old self. Elli hoped Pam's concerns were a false alarm. "Hope you're ready for some company."

"I'm always ready for company, but I know you're busy. You've been working your sweet patootie off on the Buy A Board campaign from Charlotte. So it's almost like you're here anyway."

Being here made Elli realize just how much she'd missed this place. She'd only been fooling herself that working on that project from Charlotte was the same. It wasn't. "I've missed you."

"I've missed you too, dear." Nana hugged her again, so tight that Elli found herself gulping for a breath. "Let me look at you." She stepped back and looked Elli up and down. Her silvery curls bounced as she nodded approval. "You look even prettier. I love your chic hairdo. That's a city-girl look if I ever did see one."

Elli touched her hair. The short look was new, and she was still getting used to it.

"I like the way I can see your face without all that hair hanging down around it. Shows off my blue-eyed beauty."

"You're not biased or anything," Elli teased.

"Well, you were the prettiest baby in the world. I still say you could have been on commercials, but you've done okay for yourself. By the way, that delivery of wood came, just like you said it would. Did I tell you that? I did, didn't I?"

"Yes. We spoke." Elli wondered if Nana was starting to get a little forgetful. The mail and now the comment about the wood.

"Oh, good. Yes, I do remember now. That's a lot of boards! They brought it on one of those trucks that had the forklifts on it. Good thing. Probably would've taken all day if they'd had to unload those boards one at a time."

It was true. The outpouring of support to help fix the pier shops had shocked Elli. Social media reached so many people with just a few well-placed comments and hashtags, and it seemed like anyone who'd ever driven through Sand Dollar Cove on their coastal Carolina travels wanted to pitch in to help.

"I've got good news on that front. That's how I was able to move up my trip. I've got someone coming to start the personalization on the boards. He'll be here later this afternoon. I told him he could stay in the guest quarters. I hope that's not a problem."

"Of course not. We'd already talked about it."

"That's part of the reason I came too. I didn't want you to have to get the place ready for him."

"Him?" Nana got that twinkle in her eye. "Is this a special him?"

"No. It's not like that. His name is Brody. I've only met him online. Sorry for the short notice, but he had something come up in his schedule and had to travel sooner than we'd originally planned. Since the wood was here I figured we may as well get started."

"Could be fate. I've heard about people meeting on that Internet and falling in love." Nana beamed. "It'll be great to have someone to cook for and fuss over a little. Plus, it makes me feel like I'm doing my part. All I've been doing is working on projects to restock the store. So much of the inventory was damaged when the roof caved in during that last storm. I've salvaged all that I could, but the truth is I don't really have much to start the season off for the first time in twenty years."

"We can buy some things. Or let the popsicle stand take up a little more real estate, maybe realign some of the storefront since we'll be rebuilding anyway."

"That's an idea. The popsicles do a great business. Those kids need the money more than I do."

The truth was Nana didn't need the money at all. The shop was really more of a tradition, and something to keep her busy.

Nana reached for Elli's hand. "You were such a genius to start that business. Who knew Ever-SOL-Pops would end up thriving for so many years after you started it?"

"Not me."

"The fact that it's still helping others in this town get to college, now that's a real gift, Elli. I'm so proud of you."

"I learned that from you. Giving back to the community is important. And it's not that much work for me since the last year's recipients train this year's. Plus, I like going through the essays to pick the candidates who will run it each year. It's all a pretty well-oiled machine."

"Scholarships Elli-style." She turned and motioned Elli to follow her. "Speaking of style. Let me show you what I've been working on for the shop."

Elli followed her grandmother into the kitchen, where the smell of the baked goods was so delicious that she almost felt full without so much as a bite.

The only thing Sandy Eversol did better than bake was paint. The eight-foot-long dining room table was filled with rows of sand dollars — each in a different stage of completion. Some just started, others fully painted and some already coated with a shiny protective covering. "Nana, these might be your best works yet. They're gorgeous."

"Thanks. I'm glad you like them. I tried some new designs. It's actually been quite fun. At least trying to get the inventory restocked is keeping me busy. I'm not sure if I can get enough done though. But I'm trying. I want to do my part."

"Don't be silly, Nana. You need to just relax and do what you do best. Paint and talk to customers. I'll handle the rest, and I'm happy to do it." Elli walked back out to the living room and caught a glimpse of a quilt and bed pillow on one of the couches. "Is the house a little too chilly for you this winter? I can get someone to come check the heat if you need me to."

"No." She raced over to the linens and began folding them. "It's fine. I'm really quite comfortable. The new heat and air unit they installed last year works so well. It's very efficient too. My bills are half what they used to be."

"Well, then what is all of that?" She noticed the tired look on Nana's face.

Nana shook her head and sat down on the couch, hugging the linens to her chest. "You know, the truth is, Elli, it's just been a little easier to sleep here on the couch rather than climb those stairs. My legs get to aching so bad some evenings I'd rather not make the climb."

"Are you okay?" Pam's concerns should've prepared her for this, but they hadn't. She walked over and sat next to Nana.

"I'm fine. I'm just getting older. There, I said it. I'm getting old. Things just aren't quite as easy as they once were, and especially not without your granddaddy around to take care of things."

Why hadn't she ever even considered the beach house might be too much for her grandmother? Maybe because Nana and Sol~Mate were synonymous. There was never a time this cottage wasn't part of their lives. But like she told her clients all the time: It's just a house. Home is in your heart. She helped people downsize all the time. Being in real estate was a constant upsize or downsize depending on where people were in their lifecycles. "Maybe it's time to find a place that's a little more manageable for you."

Nana looked surprised. "Wouldn't you be sad if I sold this place?"

Elli shrugged. Maybe at one time it would have felt like losing her second home, but now she knew better. Besides, that would just be selfish. "Of course not, Nana. Sol~Mate has given us a lot of wonderful memories, but the house isn't what makes your life special, it's the people you spend it with and the things you choose to do with your time that make it important. You taught me that."

"You really wouldn't mind if I moved?"

"No. Not at all." Elli was glad Nana had confided in her. This was easy to fix. "It's settled. I'll take a look and see what's listed, and pull some comps on this place. We can at least look at our options."

Nana looked so relieved. "Oh, honey, that would be great. It would be a huge burden off of me. I was talking to my friend, Janice. You know, my friend with the crazy talking bird that I play bridge with. Well, she doesn't have the old bird anymore. She moved into the retirement condos near Manteo. She's so much happier without the upkeep of her house. She's been telling me I should move there. Only I think I'd rather just be in a smaller house. I don't think I'm ready to just be around a bunch of old farts. And I really want to be here in Sand Dollar Cove."

Elli had to laugh, because compared with Nana most of the people her age were just old farts. "I think it's a good plan. I guess you'll want to stay close to the pier. Anything else on your must-have list?"

"Just a guest room, and a craft room. A wonderful room with lots of windows where I could paint the days away. I would really love that."

"Got it. Near the pier and a sunny studio to paint in."

"Actually, I don't have to be near the pier. They haven't even renewed any of the pier licenses. I'm not sure what's going on with that."

"I'm sure it's just a formality."

"You haven't been down to see the damage to the pier yet, have you?"

"I stopped by there on my way here. It does look worse in person. I'll give you that, but I'm sure they'll get that fixed. Isn't that what insurance is for?"

"Maybe you're right. I'm probably worrying for nothing, but it sure seems like a lot to fix." Nana shook her head, and the doubtful look on her face gave Elli pause.

"I'll check into it. In fact, can I get the keys to the shop? I want to stop in there and make sure things are where I remember so I can be prepared when Brody gets here, then I'll go get a closer look at everything at the pier. I need to get a plan and timeline in place for the repairs anyway."

"The keys are on the hook by the front door."

A whisper of anxiousness ran through her. Nana looking so worried and having trouble getting around made Elli regret offering to put Brody up here at Sol~Mate. She might have to reconsider and move him to Carolina By The Sea, if

Pam even had a vacancy. But he'd be here this afternoon, so she'd play that by ear.

As soon as she had a chance, she'd have a quick look down at the shop and head down to the pier to see whether there was any more salvageable inventory on the pier. That way maybe she could get Nana to slow down her production line of those painted sand dollars and take a break before she gave herself a heart attack.

~*~

Elli helped Nana get the room freshened up for their guest, and together they made such quick time of it they did a good once-over of the whole house. Nana dusted while Elli vacuumed, moving furniture to get every bit of dust and sand up, even wiping down the base molding. A stack of shipping boxes that had been broken down and tucked behind the bookcase next to the door came in handy to quickly box up some of the extra knickknacks to reduce the obvious clutter. A step they'd have to take if they were going to sell the place anyway, so why wait.

"It looks a hundred times better in here already," Nana said.

"We did good. We're a good team."

"We always were."

Bah-duup. Elli grabbed her phone from the pocket in the front of her purse and swept her finger across the screen. "Our guest is on his way. That was the driver from the airport."

"Did he fly in on the new charter?"

"Apparently so. Can't wait to hear how it was." He must have some good business on this coast to be able to afford a charter, but if it meant she didn't have to pay to get him here, that was definitely good for the budget.

It wasn't a bad deal for Brody Rankin either, because renting a room on the beach for a month or longer could get pricey, and this was one of the best spots.

Just as she put the vacuum back in the hall closet, Nana called out, "They're here. My goodness, it's a pink Cadillac limo. Have you ever seen such a thing?"

Elli joined Nana at the front door and busted out laughing. "Well, well. Looks like they bought a secondhand Mary Kay car or something. Never seen anything like it, but it's eye-catching. I guess that's good advertising."

"Something to talk about anyway," Nana said.

Brody slid out of the backseat with nothing but a duffel bag and headed for the beach house. He looked like a guy who would work with his hands and spend all his downtime on the beach. His hair was longish, and he had that sexy Adam Levine scruff thing going on.

Nana pumped her elbow into Elli's ribcage. "He's really cute."

"Shh. He'll hear you." Elli opened the front door, and she had to admit, he did fill out that red T-shirt right nice too. "Welcome. Hope you had a good flight."

"No problems at all. That little charter was sweet."

"Good to hear. They're new to the area. This is my grandmother, Sandy Eversol. I call her Nana."

Brody hitched his bag up on his shoulder and extended his hand to Nana. "Nice to meet you, Mrs. Eversol. I promise I'll be as quiet as a mouse."

"Oh, don't worry about that. Glad to have you. You can call me Nana too."

"Thanks, Nana. Great house. And I'm willing to do my part while I'm a guest in your home. Pick a night and I'll cook."

"Really? Are you teasing me?"

"No. I'm a good cook."

Nana gave Elli an impressed look. "Can't believe your girlfriend would let someone as good-looking and handy as you out of her sight for six weeks."

"I don't have a girlfriend."

Nana wrapped an arm around him like she was getting ready to weave a homespun net around the poor guy. "Let me show you your room."

Elli stood there blinking as Nana practically sprinted up the stairs like she'd just been given steroids or something. Nothing like matchmaking to get that woman a second wind.

Bless Brody's heart. He didn't stand a chance. When Nana had her mind set on something, she was relentless.

Elli waited downstairs while Nana and Brody clomped around on the top floor. That room had the best view in the house and even a small kitchenette, so he'd be pretty well set if he never wanted to visit with Nana the whole time, although he seemed to be indulging her quite nicely. Their laughter made her smile. There'd been a time when this house was always full of people. It probably got lonely for Nana now that Elli had moved off and she and her friends hardly ever stayed more than just an overnight.

Brody came down the stairs slowly, obviously letting Nana take her time. He clapped his hands together and gave Elli a wink. "I think I've had the tour. You ready to show me where the work will happen?"

"Sure. See you in a bit, Nana."

"You two have fun. It's a beautiful day out there."

"Sorry," Elli said to Brody as they walked outside. "My grandmother is always trying to be the matchmaker, but she's harmless."

"She's terrific. Reminds me of my grandmother except with a crazy accent."

"Excuse me? Are you mocking the way we talk around here?"

"Well, it's a little more twangy than I expected it to be."

"Folks say our part of the beach has its own dialect. Keeps the outsiders guessing. You'll get used to it though."

She led Brody over the dune to the workshop. He seemed at home trudging through the sand, but he came to a dead stop when they neared the building.

"*This* is your grandfather's workshop?" He glanced the length of the building and then back at her. "It's huge."

Seeing it through Brody's eyes brought a fresh appreciation for the building. Even after years of being unused except for Pops' projects, the place still looked pretty impressive. The brick exterior had held its own over the years, although the trim could use a good coat of paint. It really was kind of impressive. "They used to call this the plaza. Back in the day there were a couple shops here. That's when people frequented this end of the beach. It'd been closed for years before Pops started using it for his projects. I guess it is pretty nice."

"Nice? It's every man's dream."

Elli stifled a giggle at Brody's excitement as she pressed the numbered buttons on the keypad at the side entrance. "The code is 2020 to get inside."

"Easy enough to remember." He held his arm out and waited for her to enter. "After you."

"There's a story behind that number. My grandfather said he had 20/20 vision no matter what the eye doctor said, because the first time he laid eyes on Nana, he knew she was the woman he'd marry." She flipped the light switch and stepped inside. "That was kind of their own little *I love you*. He'd just give her a wink and say 2020." She sucked in the familiar smells of varnish and wood. "That story still makes my heart race a little. They were so in love even after so many years."

"When did he pass away?"

"About five years ago."

"Sorry for the loss." Brody stepped inside behind her and let the door close behind them. "Wow. The ultimate man cave." His green eyes flickered approval at the workbenches and neatly arranged tools. A couple chairs and a table faced a television where Pops and his buddies used to watch sports so as not to bother Nana.

"Yeah. Pops was always working on something out here. I used to love working on projects with him." She ran her hand across one of the workbenches. "The workshop is well-equipped, but if we're missing any tools I'll get whatever we need. If it's one thing I learned early on from Pops, it was that a man needs the right tools for the job."

"He trained you right." Brody walked through the space. Most of the first bay was filled with nothing but lumber. "You did good on that board campaign. Looks like a lot of wood when it's all stacked in one place."

"I thought the same thing. I'm glad they were able to fit it all inside. Just about everybody who's ever spent even one summer near our beach wanted to help restore a landmark like the pier. Only problem is now there seems to be some problem with them renewing the licenses. I'll be checking into that this week, but that shouldn't preclude us from getting started on this project."

"Sounds good." He walked over to a rack built out of PVC and flipped through the brightly colored boards, then turned to Elli. "Skimboards?"

Elli's smile beamed all the way from her heart. "Yes. My grandfather made them. He was kind of known for that design. He'd cut them out and sand them and all. Then, Nana would paint the outline of the designs and I'd fill in the colors before he put all the clear layers over them. It was so much fun working on those projects — all three of us. He made the best skimboards around." She put her hands on her hips. "I'm kind of impressed you knew what they were."

"Surprised?" Brody's shoulder bounced. "Girl, skimming was born on *my* coast."

"I always assumed it was a Carolina thing. Ya know, because our waves aren't as big for riding."

"Heck no." He pulled a bright royal-blue skimboard from the rack and wiped away the dust. "Nice work. We'll have to take some of these out and I'll show you a few things." He lifted another one out and inspected it closer. "Bidirectional board. Sweet lines."

"It's been years since I've done that, but I have to warn you I was pretty good." Her competitive nature sparked, but then her sensible self sprang forward. "Then again, I don't think we better risk you breaking an arm before we get this project done."

"You might be out of practice, but I'm not." Brody hiked himself up on the workbench. "Tell you what. How about if I get all the names done on all of these boards early, but you still let me stay the whole six weeks *and* you let me have one of these as a bonus?"

"A skimboard?"

He nodded. "Seems to me it will work out for both of us. I'll work double time and overtime to knock this job out quickly for you. And me...I'll get to play on the Carolina shores for a few weeks longer."

Elli walked over and put her hand out. "Deal."

He started to shake her hand and then pulled it back. "Oh, and we do a little skimboarding together and see just how good you are."

"You're on." She shook his hand.

"The best summer of my life might just be right here in Sand Dollar Cove."

Careful, buddy, those best-summer-evers in this town can sometimes have very disappointing endings.

CHAPTER THREE

The next morning, Elli felt like she was getting her Sand Dollar Cove groove back when she pulled on a pair of weathered Levi's and flip-flops. Even though it was March, any day over sixty degrees was good enough for flip-flops when you lived on the beach. She drove with the window down to meet Pam for breakfast at the resort. The great thing about being friends with Pam was that no matter how long they were apart, they could still pick up like no time had passed. Then again, meeting Pam for breakfast at the resort was something she could get used to doing on a very regular basis. It was a much nicer way of starting the workday than alone in her condo with her Keurig.

They dined on egg white omelets and fresh fruit smoothies in spa style.

"Did you get your cabana boy all settled in?" Pam asked.

Elli laughed. "He is hot enough to be a cabana boy, but there won't be time for playing in the sand for a while. But yes, he's all settled in."

"So he's good-looking."

"Very, in an outdoorsy I'm-going-to-hang-out-on-the-beach-and-never-be-stressed kind of way."

"Oh." Pam stopped mid-motion, her fork hanging halfway between her plate and her mouth.

"It's not that bad. He's really nice and he's eager to get started."

"No, not Brody. That." She nodded toward the door, never glancing away from it. "You are *not* going to believe who just walked in."

"Who is it? Jack?"

"No, I told you yesterday that he's in Texas. I don't really expect we'll ever see him back around here," Pam said. Elli started to turn, but Pam put her hand on Elli's arm. "Don't look, but it's you're old boyfriend."

"I don't have an old boyfriend. What are you talking about?"

Pam held her glass up and whispered. "Holden Moore."

"Holden from the best *and* worst summer of my life, Holden?"

"One and the same."

Elli spun around in her chair, then she turned back and clasped a hand over her mouth. "It *is* him. He's back? When did he get back?"

"I meant to tell you."

Her whole life seemed to be rewound like an old cassette tape...to that summer just before college. And not the good old favorite song kind of feeling either. "Is he visiting or really back?"

"He's back. For good."

"And you just forgot to mention it to me? No phone call?"

"It's not that big of a deal, is it? I mean your summer with him was a long, long time ago. I mean you're over him, right?"

"Of course, I'm over him. I was over him the moment he left this town." She turned around to catch another glimpse of him. He hadn't seen her, but he looked good. Really good. The last time she'd seen him he had more of a boyish charm in boarding shorts and was too tan for what was considered healthy these days. Today he was dressed in a suit, and those boyish good looks were now replaced with just the right amount of bulk to fill out that business suit right nicely. The two men who had walked in with him were both wearing suits too. Man, he cleaned up nice.

Pam lifted a hand in the air. "Good morning, Holden."

"Shh. What are you doing?" Elli crouched.

"Saying hello. He's a good customer. They have meetings here all the time." Pam smiled. "Sit up. He's coming this way."

"I'm going to kill you."

"You're going to thank me. It's history. Move on."

All she could remember about Holden, besides the way he looked running on the beach, was the way he kissed. Even though it had been the summer before she started college, she could remember it like it was yesterday. He'd surf all day while she worked her popsicle stand. They'd spent nearly every waking moment on the beach that summer, even lying under the stars down in the cove on her grandparents' property. It had been a magical summer.

"Good to see you this morning," Pam said. "I think you might remember my friend Elli."

Elli wished she could crawl right under the table.

His eyes registered recognition immediately. "Elli? Wow, it's great to see you. You look...you look amazing." He stared a little too long. "Are you staying in town long?"

Her palms began to sweat like a nervous teenager. "I'm here visiting my grandmother. Just for the weekend. You know. Not forever. Weren't you in Chicago, or somewhere up north?" She knew darn well exactly where he'd been. Still broke her heart remembering when he took off to move for good. In Boston for college was one thing, but the move had quickly fizzled their budding relationship.

"Boston," he said. "I was in Boston, but I'm back. I heard you're working in Charlotte."

Elli sucked in a breath. There was no denying the little zing that went through her when he spoke. She'd been so sad after he left, and bless the guys' hearts that she dated after he moved, because she measured every single one of them to Holden's standards. Not an easy act to follow.

He'd obviously been asking about her. *Stop it, Elli. It was a million years ago and surely he's married and has kids by now.*

"It's great to see you. A really nice surprise," he said. "Made my day."

"Really? I don't know why. I mean, you're the one who left in a cloud of dust. What was it you said...even a girl as cute as me couldn't hold you down in this one-horse town." She leveled a stare at him. She might not have had the chance to say anything to him after he'd left, but it felt good to at least get a little say in now.

Pam kicked her square in the shin under the table. It was all Elli could do to not shout out in pain. She pasted a grin on her face instead and tried to listen to Holden.

"Well, I might have been a little high on my horse after getting accepted to Harvard."

"You think?" Elli risked a glance over at Pam, and just as she expected she was getting the what-the-heck-are-you-doing look.

"But then you left too. I know because I came looking for you." Holden held her gaze. Only his didn't hold the daggers she hoped hers were displaying.

She swallowed, only it was hard because suddenly her throat was as dry as a powder house. She would've known if he'd come back looking for her, wouldn't she? "I never would have left if you'd stayed, but that's water under the bridge, or the pier I guess we could say." And darn if she didn't regret saying that out loud as soon as the words hit the air. And by the look on Pam's face, she wasn't too pleased about it either.

Elli felt bad for running her mouth to one of her customers like that, even if he totally deserved it.

"I've got to run. Business meeting, but I'd love to connect while you're in town. Could we? I mean, to just catch up. It's been years." He glanced at Pam. Then back to Elli. "Could I call you?"

"Of course you can call her." Pam pulled an ink pen from the top of her purse and shoved her business card across the table toward Elli. "Here, Elli, you can write your number on this." The forced smile from Pam was clear that Elli had no other option.

Elli took the pen in her hand, but for a moment she just sat there unable to even bring her own phone number to mind. Then she quickly scrawled her cell number on the card and handed it to him. *Say something.* But nothing came out. Not a single word. Not even a sound.

He flipped the card against his other hand. "Great." He took a step back. "I'll call you."

Pam and Elli sat there without a word between them, watching him make his way through the tables toward a party of six other businessmen already in discussion. Holden unbuttoned his jacket and took a seat at the large table with the rest of the men.

The last person she'd ever expected to see this morning was Holden Moore. He lifted his chin in Elli's direction as he sat.

"I'm sorry. I don't know what got into me," Elli said.

"No kidding. I've never seen you act like that."

She nodded and turned to Pam. "I was such a dork."

"You were not. He seemed kind of nervous too. Y'all are still cute together. He didn't even seem to notice you were cutting him off at the knees."

"Stop it."

"No. There was an attraction once. Y'all were kids back then, but you're both adults and single now."

"He's single?" Why did she even ask?

"Sure is. They say there's a fine line between love and hate. I don't know what that was you were spewing, but whatever it was, it was emotional. Maybe it's worth just a little exploration. Come on. What do you have to lose?"

"Don't you go playing matchmaker."

"It's just catching up on old times. Not a date. Relax and enjoy it."

Easy for her to say, she didn't feel that wave of memories tug at her like an undertow.

CHAPTER FOUR

Elli drove back to Nana's so deep in thought about Holden and their past, and today's brief encounter, that she didn't even remember taking the turn off the beach road or into the driveway at Sol~Mate.

Nana's minivan was gone, so Elli went upstairs and finished unpacking her things in the same blue dresser, as she had for as many years as she could remember coming here. The quilt Nana had hand-stitched with the Carolina lighthouses on it still looked as bright and colorful today as the Christmas she'd first given it to her. All the pictures on the wall were crafts the two of them had done together over the years. Shell art, paintings, sand art, and some finger paintings. Even the designs on the old roll-up shades on the windows had been a project. Nana had let Elli cut out little nautical flags from fabric swatches that spelled out DREAM. It had seemed like a secret spy code at the time, and that had made it that much more fun. The two of them had carefully appliquéd them to the shade and made matching pillows for the bed.

Yes, she'd miss the house, but these memories would never fade away.

One thing for sure, she was getting more and more used to not fighting the changes life had brought her way, and boy did that make things easier.

Nana sang out her arrival. "Home with groceries."

Elli took the stairs two at a time. "I'll get the rest of them."

"Thanks, dear."

Elli made two trips down to the minivan and back. "Did you buy the place out? Looks like you're ready to be snowed in for a month by the looks of this haul."

"Just a few special things I want to cook while you're back in town, and for our guest of course."

"You don't have to go to that trouble."

"You know it's no trouble at all. I love having someone to cook for."

Elli put the last bag on the counter and kissed Nana on the cheek. "You are the best. I'm going to head down to the pier to check things out."

"Okay, honey. I've got dinner in the slow cooker, so whenever you're back, it'll be ready."

"Thanks." Elli grabbed her windbreaker and headed outside. The afternoon sun was warm, but depending on how long she was gone, the walk back later could be cooler. That was the only problem with this time of the year. The temperatures still bobbled around a lot so you got used to just preparing for anybody's guess.

"See you later." Walking down the stairs, she could see how it would be hard for someone Nana's age to navigate them. It was a little tricky for her now that she was out of practice.

The sand was smooth from last night's heavy winds. Her footsteps were the only disturbance. She navigated the weathered boards that terraced their way across the steep dune. At the top, she stopped to look out to the water's edge.

It was almost eleven and the tide was all the way out. She loved low tide the best. It was when the beach was the widest and the sand bar made itself visible. She used to pretend it was her own private island.

Truth be told, the beach wasn't nearly as wide as it had been twenty years ago. Erosion was nipping away at the property. In fact, some of the folks up the beach had property lines that were now in the ocean.

But that was nature, and with time all things changed. The shift of the beach was just its way of aging, maturing into what nature had in store for it next.

Elli took in a deep breath of fresh air and closed her eyes. The tiniest inkling of spray from the ocean wafted through the air. She always felt so small compared with the strength of the ocean, but at the same time it empowered her too. Like that spray was some kind of fairy dust that made all things good.

Invigorated, she jogged down the dune to where the sand was firm. After pulling off her shoes, she laid them on top of her windbreaker to keep a breeze from whisking it away, then she rolled up her jeans and headed to the water.

The familiar texture of the sand felt good on her feet. Along the water's edge she dug her toes into the sand. The water was still icy cold from the long winter, but there was something soothing about the tide sucking at her feet, as the waves rolled in and then swept back out with just as much force, that it was worth the chill.

She kicked through the water, feeling at one with the beach again. Nana had always sworn Elli had ocean water in her veins. She tended to believe that, because she felt so alive when she was near it.

Walking back up along the line where the water met the dry sand, expired sand dollars lay among the debris and shells. She collected a stack of the sand dollars for Nana then grabbed her shoes and coat and headed on up the beach toward the pier.

Moments spent here on the beach tickled her brain. Happy times from days gone by. Some magical, and some she wished she could forget, like the year she broke her arm skimboarding. That summer with Holden too. At least the way it had ended.

The pier seemed to look worse each time she saw it. Several of the piles that had been broken off were now wedged up under the pier, making it look messy and neglected.

A few guys with four-wheelers and some ropes could haul those out and clean it up before summer came. They'd done it before.

She ducked under the yellow caution tape and made her way up the pier to where the storefronts were. At least this part of the pier was still intact, even though the entire middle section was gone.

The decades-old wood shimmered a silvery hue in the sun. The wood was so worn that it was nearly cotton smooth. The old pier had weathered years of the powerful surge of the tides here off the Carolina coast, but today the whole pier seemed to shift, feeling unsteady.

It was eerie for the pier to be empty. Even this time of year there'd normally be some guys braving the cooler temps to catch some red drum, since they usually started running pretty strong off the pier about now. Last year, someone reeled in one weighing close to ninety pounds. Sadly, it missed beating the record by only four pounds, but it was still worth some heavy-duty bragging rights.

She stood in the doorway of Ever-SOL-Pops. She'd opened that shop when she was in high school. Most people didn't even realize that the Pops in the company name was a play on her nickname for her grandfather, since he'd funded the whole start-up business. They just assumed it was for the product; the scrumptious ice pop recipes she'd perfected over two summers without ever realizing she was building something that would go on to last for years.

She and Pops together had built the sign that still hung above the door too. She'd drawn up the design to look like it was made from giant Popsicle sticks. He sawed and planed and mitered boards to look just right and then used a router with expert precision to cut out the letters just as she'd drawn them. She remembered standing at his side as the wail of that router screamed against the wood, leaving the perfect image behind. It had been such an exciting time. She and Nana had painted the sign using colors as vivid as the sweet treats she'd be selling. Each year at the end of the summer, they applied a new coat of clear to protect it. She still had that task on the season-shutdown checklist for the kids who were awarded the use of the popsicle stand to earn money for school. It still looked bright and cheerful.

The sign over Nana's shop, however, had broken free from its spot. The huge turquoise sign lay on the dock like it had passed out from too much to drink last night.

She lifted the edge of it with her foot then picked it up and leaned it gently against the side of the building. A part of the roof had peeled back over SandD's Gift Shop. Too bad it hadn't been the other way around. If the roof had been damaged over Ever-SOL-Pops, there wouldn't have been any problem. The only things in there were two freezers, and those were kept unplugged and covered up during the offseason.

Mother Nature rarely played fair though.

Nana and Pops had met on this pier. Love at first sight. This old pier was as much a part of her family tree as her cousins were.

She went inside the gift shop, but Nana seemed to have already cleared out most of the ruined inventory. Her hopes for a bounty of goodies to fill a few shelves were dashed pretty quickly. She walked back outside and held what was left of the sign against her, hugging it like an old boyfriend. The old weatherworn teal plank had seen dozens of hurricanes and winter storms, even that fire back in 1979.

Her heart felt as dark as a cloudy night sky. She might have spoken out of turn when she touted that the shops on the pier would be repaired and reopened this season. From the looks of things, she had a much bigger job in front of her than she'd thought.

She carried the sign back toward the beach. Ducking under the caution tape, she slid the sign under and pulled it behind her, with it *thump thumping thumping* with every bounce against the uneven decking boards.

Once on the sand, it was easier to drag, but she was worried about the pier. Losing it would be like losing an old friend.

It seemed like everything she knew about Sand Dollar Cove had somehow changed. Some for the better, like Pam's spa, but mostly not, and that was making her feel incredibly down. She really hadn't expected to feel this way, but then she hadn't expected to be faced with so much change either.

She dragged the sign behind her, like so many memories that she couldn't bear to leave behind. For a moment she thought about all those years ago when she'd lain on the beach for hours a day just waiting while Holden surfed every wave.

The sound of someone jogging up behind her made her turn to say hello, but it wasn't a jogger after all. It was Holden, like just thinking about the man had made him appear. And it wasn't like he was dressed for a jog.

Damning herself for thinking about him, she pushed her hair behind her ear and forced a smile. "Hi, Holden. What are you doing down here?"

"Thought I might catch up with you."

"Really."

He shrugged. "You mind?"

"No." That's what Nana would call an outright lie.

"Let me get that for you." He grabbed the sign and hoisted it under his arm like a surfboard.

That only intensified the déjà vu. "Thanks."

"Too bad about the pier."

"I didn't realize it had suffered that much damage. I'd seen the pictures on television. I thought it was mostly the decking that had gotten swept away, but even the piling and beams are a mangled mess."

He nodded slowly. "It's substantial."

"I started a Buy A Board campaign way back after the first storm of the season. I raised enough money to fix the damage to the stores and the railing at the ramp, but if the pier doesn't reopen...what good will that do? It doesn't look like they've made much progress."

He seemed to be staring at her, like he hadn't heard a word she'd just said, and that made her feel a little weird.

"It's good to see you. You haven't changed a bit."

"Sure I have. That was a long time ago."

"Not that long ago."

She tried to play it off with a shrug and picked up her pace. But she'd be lying if she didn't admit that she remembered everything like it was yesterday. Even the way his mouth had felt, tasted, when he'd kissed her the very first time under the moonlight near the second piling of the pier. She'd been nervous with her grandparents just above them in the shop. It had been like riding a wave on the morning of a hurricane. Risky, maybe even a little reckless, but exhilarating.

"You cut your hair. I like it."

She touched her hair, remembering how he'd always run his fingers through it. "You always liked it long."

"It suits you. So is your partner covering for you while you're in town?"

How did he know she had a partner?

"People talk," he said as if he could read her mind.

"He'll cover me. I haven't been down here in too long."

"So, then you're going to be sticking around for a couple weeks?"

"I think so. It's time I helped Nana get moved into a smaller place that she can manage. The stairs are tough on her, and Lord knows there are way too many of them in that huge beach house."

"Are you gonna sell the Sol~Mate?"

"We haven't gotten that far. Could always rent it out, but then that old house is getting up in years too. Not going to be long before she starts requiring some significant updating."

"True. Well, if you decide to sell we've been having pretty good luck moving properties lately. But I guess you know that. I heard you're in real estate."

"I am," she nodded. "Still licensed here in this area too."

"I'd love the chance to take you out to dinner."

That seemed to have been lobbed from left field. She hesitated.

"We have an awesome new seafood joint just up the road now. I'm making a little more money nowadays than I was back before college." He laughed. "I'll take you for something better than a Tony's Hot Dog."

"I loved those hot dogs. He isn't still open, is he?"

"Moved to the next town over to be closer to his mom, but hey, if it gets you to say yes, I'll spring for the road trip for a hot dog instead the swanky restaurant."

"I'll take you up on the hot dog. Chili and cheese."

"Just like old times."

His perfect smile made her nervous. "I guess that means you'll still be getting double onions."

With a laugh he said, "You better believe it."

Elli pointed to the old building on the cove that used to be her grandfather's workshop. "Let's put the sign over there."

Holden followed her to the side door. "I remember an interesting evening or two here."

She punched the code in the door, opened it and flashed him one of those watch-it-buster looks.

"What's all this?"

"All the boards sponsored for the pier shop repairs. They just delivered them the other day. I told you I'd done pretty well with it. This is the haul. I've got someone here to start personalizing them with the names of the sponsors." She walked over to the workbench. "This looks awesome." She tilted the board up. "Look. This is going to be great."

He set the sign down on top of one of the bundles of lumber then walked over to where she was standing. "How many of those do you have to personalize? Fifty? A hundred?"

She sputtered. "Try hundreds with an S. Nearly every one of these will be personalized."

He blinked but didn't say another word. Probably thankful she hadn't asked him to help, and he sure didn't look like he was getting ready to offer anyway.

"Thanks for carrying that."

"My pleasure." He followed her out, and she tested the door to be sure it had closed and locked then headed toward the beach.

"I forgot how great this part of the beach was." He shoved his hands into his pockets and took a jump back as the tide licked up toward his shoes. "The cove was always the best part. Maybe because it was always shut down from the public."

"To save the sand dollars." She dug her toes in the sand, and no less than a half-dozen tiny young sand dollars surfaced. "Don't need saving now. Look at 'em all."

He stooped down and put one in the palm of his hand. "I bet most people don't even know what a live sand dollar looks like. Heck, they might not know they were ever living creatures to begin with."

She shrugged. "Possible, I guess." She took the tiny creature from his hand and laid it back in the wet sand.

"I guess I'll head back. It was really good seeing you."

She watched him walk away. There were still a lot of emotions stacked up with that baggage.

CHAPTER FIVE

Elli had spent most of the morning working up the listing to put Sol~Mate on the market. The comps looked promising. At least that was going their way, only finding the perfect place wasn't going to be easy. There weren't that many places for sale in the cove. Especially not when you started trying to find something without a lot of stairs. But right now she and Nana were enjoying their time together as they sat side by side in massage chairs at the Carolina By The Sea Resort and Spa receiving pedicures.

"How's that feel?" Pam stood in the doorway holding crystal flutes filled to the top with sparkling mimosas. "I brought y'all a little treat."

"Oh, Pam. You are going to spoil us," Elli said.

"That's the plan."

Nana took a glass and lifted it to her lips. "Delightful, dear."

"You deserve it, Nana." Pam sat down in the chair on the other side of Elli. "You too," she said to Elli. "Wish I could spoil you into sticking around."

"Must be nice to be able to sit in these chairs whenever you like." Elli reached over and pushed the button to start the massage mechanism in Pam's chair.

"You can. Just pop on in whenever you have time. I wish I had more time for it myself. I'm glad y'all took me up on a visit today. Monday is always our slowest day of the week. I personally think it's nicer when it's quiet."

"But a bustling business is the sound of money," Elli said.

"I've been really lucky. A lot of the other businesses around here are struggling. I would be too if I'd kept this to just a little day spa. It's exhausting sometimes, but I knew it when I got to the point that I needed to go big or go home."

"You need to hire more help."

"I have. I've tripled my staff over the past five years."

"You need more management staff so you can take some time off. If I know you, you probably have your hand in every single tick of the clock around here."

"Guilty as charged." Pam swiped the glass of champagne from Elli's hand and took a sip, then handed it back. "I would hire someone if I could get someone like you to come work with me. Why don't you move back and partner with me. We'd have so much fun, and you're the smartest businesswoman I know."

"I couldn't stay cooped up all day. Not my style. Plus you wouldn't want me working while on a mimosa buzz. I'd be a maniac."

"Fine. Then come back and just rent a space from me for your office. You could work from here and just dawdle in the Charlotte market instead of vice-versa."

"That's a great idea, Pam. Listen to her, Elli. She's one smart cookie." Nana took another sip of the mimosa. "I think this is something anyone could get used to, Elli. Even you. Maybe we should look for a place at this end of the beach so I can treat myself to this once in a while."

"Nana's thinking of moving?" Pam's look of surprise was probably the first of many that Elli would see as people found out they were going to sell Sol~Mate.

"We've been talking, and Nana thinks a little bungalow with no stairs will be the way to go for this phase in her life. If we sell Sol~Mate, she'll have plenty of extra money for fun little getaways and spa days like this."

"I'm going to like this very much," Nana said with a tipsy grin. It looked like the mimosa was already tickling her. "I might become a frequent flyer here."

Pam clapped her hands. "This is so exciting! I'll give you a deal on a season pass. You can come as often as you like."

"Sounds divine." Nana wiggled her freshly painted toes. "I'm thinking with toes as pretty as these, it'll be flip-flop weather year round."

Pam's eyes brightened. "You know, I might just have the perfect person to look at Sol~Mate. He was just in here the other day. He was here to meet someone for lunch, and we chatted while he waited for her. Said he's been looking for a place around here. Something kind of secluded. Sol~Mate would be perfect. I don't know what his budget is, but he was driving a pretty hot car. So maybe he can afford it. I'll give him your number."

"Do that. I'd love to start showing it as soon as possible. I figure we'll have to move quickly if I want to use the summer rental option as a selling point."

"Is he single?" Nana asked.

"Yes. I believe he is," Pam said with a teasing glance in Elli's direction.

"Good, then tell him about the house *and* about Elli. It's about time Elli found a man and settled down. Preferably here in Sand Dollar Cove."

"Whatever you say, Nana," Elli said with a smile. *And wouldn't it be nice to be the age that you could pretty much do or say anything you like and get away with it.*

Oh yeah, someday she'd be like that…but for now, she had a lot of things to deal with. The first being to start the hunt for a new place for Nana and getting Sol~Mate cleared of more than fifty years of accumulated clutter.

~*~

The next morning, Elli got up with the sunrise. Something she hadn't done in months. Maybe years. Maybe since she'd lived here in Sand Dollar Cove. She rubbed the sleep from her eyes and opened the curtains.

This view begged to be on a postcard. Every part of the day brought something a little different. The tide changed the very angle and landscape of the sandy beach, and this morning the sunrise was reflecting a thousand little sparkles back at her. It looked like she could walk all the way out to the fiery sun and ride it into the sky.

Mornings were always magical in Sand Dollar Cove, and there'd been a time when Elli couldn't imagine starting her days anywhere else but here. Being here just a short while, she felt the pull of nature. This was where her heart was. It was where everything she'd ever loved had ever started...or stopped.

She poured a cup of coffee and tippy-toed past Nana, who was snoring softly on the couch. Nana looked pretty comfortable, but it kind of broke her heart to see her looking like a stranger borrowing a nap on the couch in her own house.

With the door pulled tight, she held the screen until it closed...quietly...and hiked to the beach.

The brisk morning air nipped at her nose. She pulled her hood up over her ears and plunged her hands deeper into her pockets, moving with ease through the sand toward the pier. Not for any particular reason, except that it was what she used to do every morning. It had been her routine for years. Her shoes were already filling with sand, but she didn't mind. It felt good to push her muscles; no treadmill would ever be like walking in the sand.

Dolphin played along the shoreline like a Zumba class tempting her to join in. Gulls squawked in their wake, boisterous, maybe hoping to share the fish the Atlantic bottlenose dolphin snacked on as they journeyed along the coast. Must be nice to eat and exercise at the same time.

Halfway to the pier her coffee was gone and her stomach was growling. It was a bit of a hike from the Sol~Mate to the Sunrise Breakfast Shop, but she'd been in the mood for one of their amazing breakfasts ever since she'd rolled into town. Since she was up early, why not treat herself? Once she passed the pier it was only another ten-minute walk.

She turned up from the shore to the beach road. The Sunrise Breakfast Shop was as busy as she'd remembered it. The sound of the metal utensils clanging against the cooktop sounded like an inviting promise of something Southernly and tasty as she took a seat at the counter.

A waitress placed a heavy white ceramic mug in front of her and filled it to the top with coffee without bothering to ask. "Know what you want, sweetie? Or you need a menu?"

"I'll have the Cove Cadillac and orange juice please."

The woman snickered. "You're from around here. Don't recognize you though."

"You're right. I'm Sandy Eversol's granddaughter."

"Elli? Oh gosh, you sure have grown up. How are your folks doing?" the waitress asked.

"Good. They're still living up in Virginia."

"Always did enjoy them. Glad to hear they're doing well." She scrawled on the paper. "They don't call it the Cove Cadillac anymore. Someone came in and renamed everything last year. That's the Beachcomber Breakfast now." She flipped her pencil against the order pad. "Whatever. It didn't change anything. Still two eggs scrambled with cheese, two strips of bacon below that and two biscuits for wheels, and the gravy road."

"That's it. As long as it tastes like it always did, I don't care what they call it."

"You and me both, gal. Good to see you."

And just like that she felt a little like she was back home. "Thanks." She lifted the mug to her lips, and the warm steam felt good against her cool skin. She wiggled out of her jacket, and just as she put it on the back of her chair someone took the seat right next to her.

She could hardly believe it. "You again?"

Holden set his coffee and his half-eaten plate of breakfast on the counter. "Figured there was no sense us both eating alone." He shifted into the seat. "You mind?"

"Um. No. Of course not." But she did. Sort of.

"Great. You order the Cove Cadillac breakfast?"

"I did."

"Of course you did." He smiled and swept his toast into the yolks that had run across his plate. "Remember that morning you tried to make me homemade biscuits for breakfast?"

"Oh, you're not going there, are you?"

He laughed. "I think I was scarred for life."

She swatted his arm. "It wasn't that bad."

"It wasn't that good."

"But you tried to choke it down."

"I did. But there wasn't enough orange juice in the state of Florida to get that biscuit down."

She'd forgotten about that. That little breakfast might have scarred her forever too, because she hadn't tried making biscuits from scratch since. "And you still let me try to fix breakfast for you again."

"Yep. The camping trip in Buxton. Your scrambies in the cast-iron pan were perfection."

"Haven't cooked over a campfire in years."

"Me either. I loved camping on the beach. You still know how to make those scrambies?"

"I can even make them on a stove these days. On the right bell curve I look like a pretty spectacular cook."

"You look pretty spectacular. As for the cooking?" He leaned an elbow on the counter. "I wouldn't mind finding that out."

Elli's mouth opened but nothing came out. The way he was undressing her with his eyes was borderline between flattering and creepy.

The waitress scooted her breakfast in front of her and tucked the ticket under the edge. "Take your time, sweetie. Good seeing you. Tell your grandmother Evelyn said hello."

"Will do." Although Holden's attention was a little unsettling, it wasn't totally unappreciated, but why was he still having an effect on her after all these years?

The waitress walked back over and topped off her coffee.

"Two creams," he said to the waitress and flashed a smile toward Elli.

He remembered. Now what the heck did that even mean?

Holden had been the first guy to tell her he loved her. And she'd loved him too. She'd have married him and had his babies in a heartbeat. Maybe it was for the best that he left and didn't come back. But now? Now, he should be like a stranger, but he wasn't. For some reason, that really bothered her. He was familiar, and he looked great, and he still knew everything about her.

She stabbed a fork into one of the biscuits and swept a bite into the gravy. Too bad her stomach was swirling like a washer on the spin cycle with a heavy wet quilt inside.

Holden pushed back from the counter. "I've got to get to work. I'm really glad I bumped into you. Maybe we can do it on purpose one day soon. Maybe for that hot dog."

Only he didn't even give her a chance to respond. Instead he tossed a tip on the counter and waved to the waitress and said, "Put the lady's on my tab too."

The waitress gave him a wink and a wave, and before she could say thank you, he was out the door.

CHAPTER SIX

What the heck had just happened? She'd been holding on to the anger she felt for Holden for how many years? And now she bumped into him twice and it was like her heart forgot everything it had gone through. This was not good. He was all she could think of. That somehow felt all kinds of wrong.

She added a couple of dollars to the tip, to not be outdone, then walked out the front door. She had too much swirling in her head to go back to Nana's now; besides, she was halfway to Carolina By The Sea Resort and Spa, and she needed to talk to Pam. One of those mimosas Pam loved to serve her clientele 24x7 might help calm her frazzled nerves too.

The sun felt good on her skin, and she'd broken a pretty good sweat by the time she got to the spa.

"Do you have an appointment, ma'am?" the young man behind the desk asked.

Ma'am? When the heck had she become a *ma'am*? "No. I'm here to see Pam."

"May I tell her who's here?"

"Elli."

He walked away, and Pam walked back out with him. "I didn't know you were coming by. Do you want to grab some breakfast?"

"No. I just ate."

"Did you walk down here?"

"Yeah. It just kind of happened. Why do you ask?"

She laughed. "Your hair. You look kind of like the Heat Miser from that Christmas show we used to love, but in a blonder version."

"Thanks." She tugged at her new short do to tame the windblown mess. That was the only bad thing about this short haircut. She couldn't pull it back in a ponytail.

"Well, I'm glad you stopped by. I talked to Ed this morning, the guy I thought might be interested in Nana's beach house. He's so excited to see it. He'd already found a few others he was going to look at, but I told him to stop the process until he talked to you. Can you meet with him tonight?"

"Absolutely. I can make time for that. Thanks, Pam." Timing was everything, and if opportunity was going to knock this quickly it had to be meant to be.

"No problem. He's super nice. It'd be great to get some folks that are our age moving in to this town. Seems like everyone who's come lately is retiring. Don't get me wrong, the blue-haired and retired with cash to spend are great for business, but not so much for fun or just making new friends." She sat down at her desk and started typing on her laptop. "I'll just message him real quick." Her nails clicked and clacked away. Then she looked up. "Great. He'll meet you at Breakers at six."

"Can you have him e-mail over the listings he's interested in? I'll pull them. That'll give me an idea of what he's got in mind."

Pam typed a couple more lines. "Yep. He's e-mailing them to me right now."

"Great. Perfect timing."

~*~

Elli had been sitting at the bar at Breakers only long enough to get her glass of wine when a man walked up to her and said, "You must be Elli."

"I am."

"Easy to figure out. You're the only lady at the bar."

Ed Rockingham was good-looking. Older then her. Probably in his forties but with longish hair and that rugged black T-shirt kind of look about him.

She turned to shake his hand. "Nice to meet you, Ed."

"Thanks for meeting me. Pam said you're the best real estate agent around."

"She might be biased. Pam and I go way back. I have to warn you, I'm the best in Charlotte, but I don't sell much around here — although I do know Sand Dollar Cove like the back of my hand. I promise you I'm a good listener and I'll help you find the right place for you. It's kind of my specialty."

"I think I'm most interested in the one Pam says you haven't officially put on the market yet. The one in the cove."

"It's the prettiest piece of property on the beach. The view is unbeatable, and it's private beachfront so you don't have to deal with tourists or parking issues."

"That sounds perfect."

"It kind of is. Pam forwarded me your list of houses. I've already researched them and set up appointments for tomorrow.

Ed threw a twenty on the bar. "Come on. You haven't eaten yet, have you?"

"No, but—"

"I'm starved. Grab your drink, we can talk over dinner."

"You don't have to buy me dinner."

"I don't have to, but I'd rather not dine alone. You coming?"

She jumped off the barstool and started to join him, then went back and grabbed her glass of wine and double-stepped to catch up with him.

"Two, please," Ed said.

The girl marked a table off her grid, grabbed two menus and burst into a grin when she turned and saw Elli. "How are you? I didn't know you were in town."

"Just got here the other day."

"How are things in the big city?"

"Things are going great."

"I'm so glad to hear that. Tell your grandma we miss her. She hasn't been in to see us in quite a while."

"I will." It bothered Elli to hear that Nana wasn't getting out and about like she had been. A hair appointment or two was one thing, but she used to come here for dinner frequently. Just how long had all this been going on? Sometimes things had a way of putting you back where you belonged, or where you were needed. She was suddenly very glad she was in Sand Dollar Cove, and if she was going to be here for a little while, a little side job was a nice little extra.

The waitress seated them near the window. As the sun set, lights that dotted the edge of the dock all the way to the gazebo came on and cast a magical glow against the darkening ocean and sky.

"So, I take it you have family here," Ed remarked.

"I spent nearly every summer here. It's a great town. Good people. How did you find our little piece of heaven?"

"I've always loved the Outer Banks. Spent a lot of time there as a kid. Then a friend of mine came to the spa here. I met her for lunch one day since I was nearby. Kind of liked what I saw." He nodded. "So here I am."

They ordered dinner, and when the waitress brought their drinks to the table, Ed lifted his in the air. "To finding me a place where I can relax and enjoy the sounds of only the ocean."

Elli raised hers and gave him a nod. "We can do that." She took a sip of her drink and found herself a little surprised that she was kind of captivated by this guy. He looked a little wild-eyed on the outside, but there was something gentle and kind about him that she liked. "What do you do?"

He paused for a moment. "Well, I'm on the road a lot, so I'm really looking for somewhere I can come home to and feel like I'm rooted before heading back out. Peace and quiet and a helluva view."

"It's a couple hours to the nearest commercial airport from here, but we have a new private charter that's not too terribly expensive."

"That can work. It's time I slowed down a little and figure out a way to find some balance. Enjoy things besides work."

"Sand Dollar Cove is a great place to find work-life balance. It's probably my favorite place on earth."

"If it's your favorite place, why don't *you* live here?"

"That's a good question." And it was, because there was never a moment that she'd felt that way about Charlotte. "There are a lot more houses to sell in the city."

"More, huh?" He nodded slowly. "I get it. *More* drives a lot of people."

"More customers keep a paycheck coming in." His words kind of caught her off guard though. She'd never thought of herself as someone who needed more. Why did she all of a sudden feel like she needed to defend herself?

"I think I'm ready for less." He sucked in a breath of air and made it look as sweet as cotton candy. "Less noise, less trouble, less traffic, less mess. A few less people is okay with me too."

His smile was gentle, and his eyes danced when he spoke. He'd fit right in around here. "Well, Ed, I think you've come to the right place."

Dinner conversation was easy. As they each plowed into a shared slice of the famous seven-layer chocolate cake, Elli got the last of the details she felt she needed to make their house hunt a success.

"I think I have everything I need to get us going. Let's find you that perfect place."

Ed reached across the table and patted her arm. "Thanks. I appreciate you dropping things to meet with me so quickly. I have a good feeling about you. Pam. This town. I'm pretty sure you're going to find me exactly what I need."

Elli had almost forgotten how different it was selling property in a beach town than in the city. Even the customers were easier to take. A refreshing change of pace.

"Hi, Elli."

She straightened. The way Holden said her name stabbed at her heart.

"Seems like we're running into each other everywhere these days," he said.

She hadn't even heard Holden walk up. "Seems so." She turned and tried to look pleasantly surprised.

"Who's your friend?" Holden asked with a raised brow, and although the words came out polite enough, there was a little edge to them that made Elli uneasy.

"Oh, sorry. Where are my manners? Holden Moore. This is Ed Rockingham."

Ed lifted his hand from Elli's arm and reached out to shake Holden's. "Hey, man."

Holden shook his hand. "Yeah, Elli and I go way back. Great gal you've got there."

"No, Holden," Elli said shaking her head profusely. "Ed and I are just here on business. I'm helping him shop for a house."

"Sorry. Just assumed." Holden's face flushed pink. "Well, the compliment still holds. She's a great gal."

"I'm finding that out," Ed said, and that glance he just gave her felt a little like a flirt. Or was that wishful thinking? And had Holden been just a teensy bit jealous? That wasn't such a bad feeling either.

"Yeah, well I'm meeting a client here too," Holden said. "Just wanted to say hello."

Elli smiled, and there was an awkward moment as Holden backed away. "Sorry, that was a little weird."

"Old boyfriend?"

"Like college-days old. Doesn't-even-count old."

"Says you," Ed said with a smirk.

And I would know. "I was thinking I could pick you up at nine tomorrow, so we could take a look at the houses on your list. I picked out a few others that I think might be good options too."

"Actually, I've got something tomorrow, so can we plan on Thursday? Is that okay?"

"Absolutely. Thursday it is."

His smile was relaxed. "And let's look at the beach house on the cove first. I have a feeling it's going to be the one to compare everything else with. I might not even have to look at anything else."

"You got it. I'll arrange everything."

"I'm staying at Carolina By The Sea. I don't mind meeting you somewhere on this end of the beach, if you'd rather."

"Nope. I'll meet you in the lobby. Pam serves the best coffee around."

~*~

When Elli got back to the beach house, she was surprised to see another car sitting in the driveway. Nana hadn't mentioned having company tonight. Maybe Brody had chosen to rent one.

The driver's door opened, and Holden stepped out. "Sorry about earlier," he said as he walked over. "Didn't mean to make it awkward for you. I didn't realize you were on business."

"Is that why you're here? Oh, Holden, you don't need to apologize. It was fine. An honest mistake."

"Actually, it wasn't such an honest mistake. I hadn't even planned to go in there until I drove past and saw your car. I wasn't there for a business meeting. And I'm not here to apologize. I'm here because seeing you again ..." His head lolled back. Following a deep exhale he said, "I've wanted to see you again. For so long. When I moved back and folks said you hardly ever came around anymore I was sorry to hear it, because you were one of the main reasons I returned to Sand Dollar Cove. And then I convinced myself that it was just old stuff and put it aside. But I have to tell you, after seeing you...talking to you...All those feelings from that summer we spent together, they are still as strong now as they were then."

"That was a long time ago."

"Not that long ago." His eyes held hers. "Best summer of my life."

"Somehow I doubt that."

"I had no idea how much I was going to miss you until I was gone."

"That's sweet." But she wasn't buying it. She didn't know what he was trying to prove to himself, but she wasn't going to let herself get hung up in that old net again for anything.

"I'd like to see you while you're in town."

"I'm going to be really busy. I'm just trying to tie up some loose ends and find Nana a new place to live. Figure out what's going with her store. Get her all set. I don't even really know how long I'll be in town."

"You didn't feel a thing?"

Had she been that transparent, or was he that egotistical? The truth was she'd been swirling those old memories around too. But this time she wasn't going to think with her heart, she was going to use her head. "I—" And her head was telling her to get the heck off that subject. She pulled her hands up on her hips. "You mean to tell me after all this time you're not married with a couple of kids? I seem to remember something about you wanting a little boy to teach how to surf and fish."

"Still do. And no. Haven't ever married. You?"

"Married and divorced. It wasn't meant to be. He's a nice guy, just not the right one for me. We're still friends."

"That's unusual, but I'm not surprised. You were always so easy to get along with."

Not easy enough, as she recalled. "It's all good."

He let out a long, slow breath. "I know this is going to sound kind of ridiculous, but when I saw you with that guy ..."

"It's fine. You didn't harm our business at all. Really, please don't give it another thought."

"I didn't like it."

"What? That doesn't make sense. What was there to not like?"

"I wanted to fight to get you back."

That put her back on her heels a little. "I'm not yours."

"That's what I didn't like. I don't think I've ever felt that way before."

"I'm not sure if I should be flattered or concerned."

"Flattered, I hope. I'm not the jealous type. I just know how special you are. I screwed that up when I had the chance the first time. But I'm a man now. A man who won't let that kind of love slip away again. I'd love it if you'd give me another chance. Now that I'm more grown up and can really appreciate you."

Her heart fluttered, although her head was telling her to calm the heck down. What he said was sweet. Absolutely. Even kind of romantic, but she was not in the market for a relationship and darn sure not for one with someone who'd already broken her heart before. A do-over of that part of that summer was definitely not in her plans. And there was Nana. She was the priority right now.

"I'm not sure that's a good idea, Holden."

"How about dinner? Tomorrow night? My place. I cook an awesome lasagna."

"You remember my weakness for Italian food?"

"I remember everything about you, Elli."

He stepped closer, and now it wasn't just her heart teaming against her. Her knees suddenly felt like Jell-O on a warm day.

Well, truth be told, she hadn't forgotten one thing about him either, but she wasn't up for another heartbreak like that in her lifetime.

"Please. One dinner. If you never want to get together again, I'll honor that. I promise." He bent his knees a little to get down to her level and look her eye to eye. "Please?" And there was that smile. "Seven?"

She felt herself sink under the pressure of the invitation. "Fine. One dinner."

He pulled her into a friendly hug and held her for nearly a four-count. "You're not going to regret this. I'll pick you up." He turned and left, probably to be sure she didn't have time to back out.

And she was already regretting it.

CHAPTER SEVEN

Elli tossed and turned all night long. First, waking up in a sweat from the good memories from that summer with Holden, and then in a panic from the bad ones, followed by crazy, mixed-up dreams of worst dates ever. Probably a premonition for tonight's dinner with him.

Why had she said yes?

She got out of bed and pulled on a pair of jeans and a T-shirt. She plodded out to the kitchen at six, and Nana was already up, sitting with a mug of coffee in front of her.

"Good morning, dear. You're up early," she said.

Elli poured a cup of coffee and joined Nana at the table. "Didn't sleep last night."

"Is everything okay?"

She shrugged. No sense telling her about Holden. She sure didn't want to talk about that. "I was just excited about house hunting for you. I'm going to pull some listings this morning."

Nana looked around. "There's a lot of stuff here to move."

"You got that right. But we can just move what you want to move and donate the rest if you want. Don't let it worry you."

"I think downsizing is good. Maybe we could do a yard sale."

Doubtful. She wasn't much on yard sales, and who was going to come? "It'll be fine," she said just to reassure her. No one else in this town needed Nana's stuff any more than she did, but she'd let her hang on to that thought for now and then just handle it.

"I thought I'd make chicken pot pie tonight. Your favorite, and I thought Brody might like it too."

"You'll have to save me some. I have something to do tonight."

"Really? Like a date?" Her eyes danced with mischief and hope.

"No, Nana. Not a date." Nana always did seem to have an intuition about this stuff. Maybe it was a date, but she'd decided it was more of a closure meeting. Putting that whole mess behind her. "Just catching up with some people in town. I won't be late, but I'll grab dinner while I'm out."

"A date wouldn't be so bad, you know. You're too young to be working so hard, and too old to still be single."

"Well, then I'm just out of luck, aren't I?" She'd already decided she wouldn't tell Pam or Nana about her dinner with Holden so she wouldn't have to listen to all the questions they were bound to have. Besides, she didn't have any answers to those questions.

No. Some things were better left quiet. It would have been even better if she'd just said no to begin with. She'd fallen under his spell, but that wouldn't happen again. They'd do dinner. Just friends. One night to get him out of her system and her out of his. Over and done and then everything would be fine.

The only trick was going to be getting away with Nana not seeing that it was Holden picking her up tonight. She hadn't quite figured out how she was going to pull that off yet.

Brody walked in, and Nana looked like she was having a fan-girl moment. "How are you? Can I get you some sweet tea? A snack?"

"No, ma'am. Thanks." He turned his attention to Elli. "I did some sample boards."

"I loved the one you did that was on the workbench. It was perfect."

"Oh, you saw that? It was just a test run. I did the first twenty names in a couple different styles with the router bits your Pops had. You want to come down and see which you like best? I'm going to need some new bits. Those have seen better days, but it'll give you an idea of what your options are."

"That would be terrific. You want to grab some breakfast first?"

"No. I'm good. If you have time now we can finalize that decision and I can let you know which bits to buy. Should be smooth sailing from there."

"Let's do it." She rinsed out her coffee cup and met Brody on the front deck. They walked down to the shop down the lane instead of the beach.

He'd cut the straps on the lumber, and now there were several boards lying across sawhorses.

"I'm not sure exactly what you promised. I couldn't find the details on the campaign online anymore. So I did some with just one sponsor name, but then I was thinking that putting multiple names on each board might give you more flexibility in how you use these for all of the repairs? Plus, it kind of looks impressive with the names side by side. What do you have in mind?"

He handed her a carpenter's pencil.

She twisted the big squared-off pencil in her hand. "It's like a first-graders pencil. Yeah, so what they were promised was their name prominently displayed on a board used in the renovation. So, we can do multiple names on the boards if you think that will work better. I hadn't really thought about that. I ordered a board for every donation."

"Come take a look."

She stepped up next to him and looked at the different designs. "I really like the one with the multiple sponsor names together with the sand dollar in the middle. Did you do that freehand?"

He nodded. "It's kind of stylized, but the best I could do."

"I love it. We have a lot of them to do, so keeping it simple will be better. I wouldn't change a thing. I kind of like the one that looks more freehand than the perfect Times Roman letters. What do you think?"

He took the pencil from her, used a T-square to draw two straight lines, and sketched out her name. Then he picked up the router and pushed it against the wood, and for a moment Elli was just twelve years old again, standing by Pops' side here in the shop. She'd loved hanging out with him.

The router screeched, and the smell of wood filled the air. Brody shut down the router and blew the sawdust away. "Like this?"

Her name, *Elli Eversol*, gleamed back at her. It was as perfect as if Pops had been here to do it himself. "Yes! Even better. Relaxed, but clear and legible." She clutched his arm and let out a little squeal in excitement, and when she looked up at him and he smiled back, the kindness behind his green eyes seemed to touch her soul.

"Good, then I think we have a plan."

She let go of him and looked away, feeling a bit awkward for the long stare. His biceps seemed to wink at her as he put the tools away. Elli pushed the unexpected attraction aside.

"Great. Yeah, I'm just going to go back up to the house. I have so much to get done today. If I'm going to get to town and back I better get going because I have someplace to be at six." *Like he even needed to know that? Just quit talking, Elli.*

"Cool. I'm going to knock a few more of these out. I'll catch you at the house later." He tucked the pencil over his ear.

She skedaddled toward the door, stopping one last time to watch him move easily among the tools. She was lucky to have his help.

~*~

At 5:45 that evening Elli was doubly thankful for Brody's arrival at Sol~Mate. Not only had he already made a plan to get the work that she needed done in record time, but also right now he was in the kitchen showing Nana how to make fish tacos out of the frozen mahi-mahi she had in her freezer. He swore he learned how to season them to perfection from the locals while surfing off Cabo. That seemed to impress Nana, and she'd put off making her famous chicken pot pie until Elli would be home to eat with them.

Elli had no idea if Brody was making up the story or not, but if it kept Nana occupied while she slipped away with Holden...she was all for it.

One less worry for her. If fairy godmothers came in chilled-out beach-bum handsome-guy bodies...she'd swear she'd just met hers.

At just before six she slipped out the front door to meet Holden. He was right on time, pulling into the driveway as she took the last step down from the house.

He jumped out of the driver's seat and ran to open the passenger door for her. "You look beautiful."

"Thank you."

He shut the door and jogged around the front of the car. A quick three-point turn in the drive and they were headed into town, and Nana hadn't seen a thing. Elli's nerves began to tingle from the anticipation as he drove along the main beach road.

She had to admit she was duly impressed when he pulled up to the one gated community in Sand Dollar Cove. A new area, it hadn't been there just five years ago, but as more and more people discovered their little town this was where the exclusive who had money to afford new custom homes but didn't care about being on the water were building these days. They'd even put in bike routes and a crossover to the beach. A pricey solution to beach access.

"We're here," he said.

"It's lovely." Holden's house sat high on a dune. The light color stucco exterior gave it a sandcastle look. Houses that were taller than they were wide always tended to look grander, and this one didn't disappoint.

As they stood in the cone of porch light, a memory ruffled through her mind like wind on water. Moments, close like this when he'd kissed her goodnight under the porch light at Nana's and Pops'. She pulled her drifting thoughts together as he invited her inside.

An enticing aroma of garlic and herb-rich sauce dominated the air. "Oh my gosh, I think I just landed in Italy. It smells like heaven in here."

"Told you I bake a mean lasagna."

"If it tastes even half as good as it smells, you're getting a blue ribbon from me."

"I'd settle for a second chance." His gaze held hers. "Come on in. Everything is ready."

She followed him inside. Decorated in the natural colors of the sand and water, it was clean and modern, maybe bordering on an unlived-in look, but beautiful just the same. Across the living room a wall of sliding glass doors opened out to the deck. She stepped outside. There was a water view from up here. She was pulled toward it. "I hadn't realized you had a view from this side of the street."

"Only from the houses up on this ridge." On the deck a table was set for two with hurricane lanterns gently lighting the area. The decking was a shimmering sandy-textured concrete that gave her the feel of being right on the beach.

He'd obviously gone to a lot of trouble. "Can I help?"

"Everything's ready, but you can help me carry dinner out. I thought we'd eat out there." She took a covered casserole dish from him and carried it outside. The table was set as perfect as if a Girl Scout were going for her first Etiquette & Manners Badge.

He was right behind her with a glass bowl filled with a beautiful salad in one hand and a basket with what, from the smell of it, must be fresh buttered garlic bread.

"Go ahead and have a seat. I'll just grab the wine."

She sat down feeling a little surprised by the rush the attention was giving her. She hadn't expected this. In her mind it would be a quick dinner. No fuss.

He came back out and poured them each a glass of wine.

She took a sip. "Nice."

"It's local. Guy down in Currituck County. Who knew we could do sophisticated wine around here? Made a believer out of me."

"I'm impressed." She took another sip and set her glass down. "You've gone to a lot of trouble tonight."

"I wanted it to be a perfect night."

His smile was easy, and that wall she'd built around herself seemed to be as unsteady as the pier these days.

"In fact," he said, "if I timed this right, the sunset should give us a floor show in about twenty minutes, so dig in."

They sipped wine, ate, and made small talk. Holden's phone beeped. He reached for it, hit a button and then took her hand. "Come on. That was my phone reminding me of the sunset time."

Elli dapped her lips with her napkin and followed him to the deck rail. "Let me grab my wine."

"I'll get it."

She settled in at the rail, and then he was right behind her, handing her the glass from behind her. She held the glass in both hands. His body felt warm standing behind her with both arms stretched forward on either side of her. If he weren't so tall he'd have been able to rest his chin on her head, he was so close, but it felt good. Strangely familiar and for a moment it was like she was years younger, experiencing a sunset with him for the first time.

He leaned down, speaking gently into her ear. "Do you remember that first sunset? Jockey's Ridge."

She nodded. "I do. I couldn't tell if it was the sunset or the magic of the ridge that night."

He seemed to breathe in the scent of her. "I think it was both." He ran his hand up and down her arm.

The shiver from his touch made her inhale.

"And you," he said stepping from behind her to beside her, leaning in close.

"Three ..." he said.

It was just like that first time all those years ago when they'd counted it down as the sun dropped below the horizon.

"Two …" she said along with him.

"One," they said, and he moved in ever so slowly and put his lips to hers.

She'd known where he was going. She'd lived it once before. She could have turned away, kept it from happening, but she didn't. Couldn't, really. As his warm mouth met hers, she raised her hand to his cheek, drinking in the kiss and letting it last as long as it would.

"No." He turned away and looked toward the ocean. "No. I was wrong."

She stood there, her pulse racing. No? She couldn't imagine that he hadn't felt the same thing.

His voice was soft. "That ridge had nothing to do with that feeling that night. I felt the same thing just then."

Well, two could play that game. "Oh. I get it. So that kiss. It was for science? Just a test."

"Absolutely. I mean if we were sitting on information about love and sunsets on Jockey's Ridge, we owe it to the region to share that. Strictly from a tourism perspective, of course."

Thank goodness he'd lightened the mood, because moments ago she wasn't sure whether to run all the way home or go in for another kiss and throw all caution to the wind. "I totally get it."

"One problem."

She was almost afraid to ask. "What's that?"

"One is not a representative sample."

"I was afraid you were going to say that." Well, hoping was more like it. "Maybe we should finish eating before our food is completely cold."

"Good idea." He walked over and pulled her chair out for her, then he sat down.

With the kiss out of the way the conversation came more easily.

They finished dinner and cleared the table outside. "It's still early. Want to go for a walk on the beach?"

She rubbed her stomach. "I need to walk off that lasagna. Not that I'm complaining. It was worth every bite. You really are quite a cook."

"Thank you. I'm glad you liked it." He grabbed two windbreakers from the closet and handed her one.

She pulled it on, the sleeves hanging a good ten inches beyond her hands. "My hands will be warm."

"I planned on holding one of them anyway."

They walked along the beach, and it didn't take long to warm up as they hiked, just enjoying the quiet of the night. A million stars twinkled above.

Holden broke the comfortable silence. "There's a full moon on the fourth. Is it too soon to ask if you'll join me for a walk on the beach that night?"

"You mean like a date?"

"Or like a walk. I remember how you use to love the phases of the moon."

"Still do. The moon. The tides. The beach. It's part of who I am." If she really believed that, then why did she live inland? Maybe it was time to reevaluate things. First things first though, like slowing this freight train down. Things were moving way too fast on this reckless course. "I'll have to check my calendar and get back with you. I have a hundred things going on right now."

"Okay." He squeezed her hand, like he was sure she'd clear her calendar for him. "It'll be nice. Ready to head back?"

She spun around, and he fell in step with her. Going back, the breeze was in their faces, and her nose stung from the chill.

Being gone for so long, she wasn't exactly sure where they were on the coastline to know where to turn in the dunes to get back to his house. Things had changed a lot over the past few years. The walk back seemed a lot longer.

"Right here," he said pointing to a small cluster of lights atop a pole that looked like a miniature lighthouse.

He stopped her just before they climbed the steps to cross back over the road.

"Elli, this has been really nice."

"It has. Thank you. I enjoyed it."

He took her hands into his and faced her. "Damn, I've missed you," he said leaning his forehead to hers.

Her lips trembled as she tried to take a breath to steady her racing heart. Why was it so easy to fall back into an old routine? It was like muscle memory. She knew better, and she'd come here with absolutely no intention of falling into his trap. He'd broken her heart into a million pieces, and yet here she was letting him reel her in again.

She couldn't allow Holden Moore to have as much a hold on her heart right this minute as he had all those years ago.

"You are such a sweetheart." He dropped another kiss to her lips. Quick, gentle and sweet. "Let's get back to the house before you freeze."

If he thought that tremble was from the temperature out here, he was sorely mistaken.

CHAPTER EIGHT

When Holden dropped Elli back off at Sol~Mate after midnight, she was in a state of confusion. The early night she'd planned had ended up in a very long and unexpected chain of events. And the last kiss he'd laid on her before getting out of the car was just as toe-tingling as the first. It was all she could do to walk, not run, from the car.

Her grip was firm on the handrail; a splinter was the least of her worries compared with tumbling down the stairs or — worse — falling for Holden. The wine, the moonlight, that goodnight kiss had her feeling a little on top of the world and wobbly all at the same time.

As she took the last step and headed for the front door, she almost had a heart attack when the rocking chair squeaked just a few feet away.

"Sorry. Did I scare you?" Brody rocked forward and then back, pitching a piece of popcorn in the air and catching it in his mouth, then slugging back a sip of beer. He'd caught that piece, but there was evidence that he wasn't too good at it though, because there was a lot of popcorn on the deck all around him.

"Where'd you find that?"

"The popcorn? Nana popped it for me before she went to bed. I guess I'm still on West Coast time. I'm wide awake."

"I meant the Internet connectivity. Is that an iPad? Are you on the Internet?"

"Oh, there for a second I thought you were calling me out for drinking a beer."

"Hardly. If Nana hasn't mentioned it, she keeps the refrigerator downstairs stocked with it. She swears it prevents kidney stones. Frankly, I think she just loves beer. Help yourself."

"Cool. Oh, and the Internet. I brought it along."

"You don't seem the type."

"Oh, you have me all figured out?"

"Apparently not. Maybe I can hitch a ride on your Wi-Fi if you don't mind?"

"Anytime."

"Well, I guess I better get to bed." She reached for the front door.

"You were gone a long time for what was supposed to be a quick night out. Turned out to be a pretty hot date, I guess?"

There was that word. *Date*. Why did it make her want to turn and run? And although she'd convinced herself it was not a date, it sure as heck had turned into one. A really good one.

She walked over and sat in the rocker next to Brody's. "It was a good night."

"Cool. Who is the lucky guy?"

"Someone I met here on this very beach a long, long time ago."

"Summer love," he sang it out. "Nothing finer."

"Nothing can break your heart as fast either."

"Sounds like experience talking."

"Been there. Done that."

"But you're not a little girl anymore. You seem like you have a good head on your shoulders. I'm sure it'll be fine."

She plunged a hand into his bowl of popcorn. "I hope you're right." She tossed a piece of popcorn high in the air and caught it in her mouth.

"Sweet." Brody looked impressed.

"You need some practice," she said pointing at the popcorn scattered around the deck. "Hope you're better at skimboarding. 'Night." She went inside and headed up to her room.

She brushed her teeth, changed into her pajamas and climbed into bed only to get right back up to open the window. She'd need an extra blanket, but she needed the sound of the ocean tonight. The old chest at the foot of the bed would have an extra one. As she lifted the heavy lid, the welcome smell of the old cedar was nice. She used to keep her most treasured items in this chest over the summer. The quilt was folded neatly on top. Taking it out, she caught a glimpse of the old boxes of memories. She was so tempted to go through them, but half of those memories were from her days with Holden. Better to not dwell on the past. She wasn't that little girl anymore.

~*~

The soft murmur of voices rose from downstairs, pulling her from slumber. She squinted as the sun poured through the open window. The gulls calling to each other as the waves crashed was soothing. And even though she'd been up late, she felt ready and raring to go this morning.

She slipped on a pair of jeans and a long-sleeved T-shirt.

Elli wasn't halfway down the stairs before the smell of sausage hit her. When she rounded the corner, Brody was sitting at the kitchen table.

"Thought you'd be fast asleep. On Pacific Time and all," she said.

"Nope. Woke up with the sun. Already been out on the beach this morning. Great sunrise here."

"The best," she agreed.

"Sure is," Nana said. "My husband and I fell in love watching those sunrises. What kind of eggs can I make you this morning, Elli?" Nana was always chipper this time of the day, and she looked ten years younger this morning. Having someone to fuss over suited her.

"Whatever you're fixing for you and Brody is fine with me."

Brody was sipping orange juice while Nana stood vigil over the frying pan with a spatula in her hand. "Over medium all the way around then."

"Smells great," Elli said. "Been a while since I've had your breakfast." Elli grabbed napkins and utensils and set the table. "My grandmother happens to fry the best eggs in the world. She has a knack for making those edges just perfectly crispy. I swear no one does it better."

"Maybe I should have three instead of just two then," he said.

"You got it, sport," Nana said. And she looked so happy this morning. Elli hadn't ever really thought about Nana getting lonely out here, but certainly, especially in the off season, it would get that way.

"If it's not too much trouble," Brody added.

"Got to keep the help's strength up, don't I?"

"Careful now. I might be tempted to stretch out the job if you treat me too nice."

Nana laughed. "Somehow I don't think you're the type." She snapped her fingers. "I'm ready for Brody's plate."

Elli handed it to her so she could fill his plate with the fried eggs, sausage and three points of toast. Elli slid the plate in front of him then got the homemade apple butter out of the fridge and set it on the table.

"You go ahead and start there. We'll catch up," Nana said.

The old cast iron skillet sizzled and popped as Nana finished cooking their eggs, then they both sat down and joined Brody.

"This breakfast is amazing," Brody said.

Nana's eyes danced. "This is a good morning."

Elli finished hers first. She got up and topped off Nana's and Brody's coffees. "Either of y'all need anything while I'm up?"

"No, thank you," Nana said. "Where are you all in a rush off to this morning, Elli?"

"I'm going to run into town and get the couple of things that Brody needs and get your business license and permits in order."

"That would be a relief. I don't really understand what the holdup is on all of that."

"Well, I'll get it all sorted out. Don't you worry." She put her dishes in the sink and kissed Nana on the cheek. "I'll see you later this afternoon."

"I left the information on the router bits I need on the table next to the door," Brody said.

"No problem. Anything else you need?"

"That should do it. I'm going to head on down to the shop and get started." Brody threw his T-shirt over his shoulder and whisked out the door and down the stairs.

"He's a nice man," Nana said. "He reminds me of your grandfather a little. So full of energy." Her lips spread into a gentle smile. "I never could get him to just sit and take it easy."

"You're the same way. You were a perfect couple."

"We were. He was romantic too. I don't think there are many men as romantic as your grandfather."

No. Nana was probably right, but after last night Holden might be a close second.

~*~

Elli had never had a reason to come down to the new town municipal building before, but now she knew why the locals called it the Taj Mahal. It looked a bit out of place compared with the rest of the town. The building was where the old elementary school had once been. They'd torn down the eyesore and put up a new structure. It was a beauty for sure, but it looked like it belonged somewhere like Palm Beach rather than Sand Dollar Cove. It had all the beauty that a beach building in a fancy tourist town should have, right down to the fancy carved doors with the town's emblem and cool brass handles that had sand dollars cast into them. Those had to have cost a pretty penny.

She went inside and followed the arrows to a small office down the end of the hall labeled with a paper sign that read Permits. That seemed a lot more like Sand Dollar Cove casual.

"Good morning. I'm Elli Eversol. I need to get some permits straightened out."

"Sure, Miss Eversol. What can I help you with?"

"Well, my grandmother is Sandy Eversol and she has run the shops on the pier, but she said she was having trouble renewing her permits this year. I thought I'd come down and handle it for her while I'm in town."

"Oh." The young woman's face skewed. "Ya know, I'm not going to be able to help you on that just yet."

"Why not?"

"Well, that's still under discussion. The town hall meeting is tonight though, and the decisions will be made following that session."

"What kind of decisions?"

She leaned across the counter. "Look, I really doubt the pier is going to reopen. It's been a money pit for this town over the last ten years, and we're just going further into debt. Can you believe they haven't even been able to insure the pier the last few years? I liked to die when I heard that. I have a feeling they are going to have to finally bite the bullet and shut it down. It's just not safe."

It totally took her off guard. Close down the pier? They couldn't do that.

"But that pier is part of the charm of this town. It's the biggest tourism draw we have."

"I know. It's such an awful situation. But that's why they brought in that high-paid commissioner guy to make some big changes. I don't know what he'll be able to do, but you know I don't make the decisions. I'm just a clerk. Anyway, you probably want to attend the meeting." She leaned down and took a flyer from a folder and handed it to her. "Here's the information on it. It's a special meeting set up just for that."

"Well, I'm shocked no one is talking about it. This is awful." Elli snatched the paper from the girl's hand and then pasted a smile on her face. "I'm sorry. I know this isn't your doing. It's just frustrating. I'm actually really thankful you filled me in."

"Sorry to be the bearer of bad news."

Elli walked out wondering why Pam hadn't mentioned it to her. It had to be the talk of the town, or maybe like always this town just assumed someone would find a way to keep things the same...the way they always did. Only this time she had a feeling it might be bigger than anything the town could turn around, especially if safety was the deciding factor.

If the pier didn't reopen, Nana would be crushed.

Elli had to be at that meeting, and if there was anyone who could talk some sense into this town and a new commissioner it was her. She'd been the head of the debate team, and she loved this town as much as the people actually born here. Snippets of compelling arguments fought for attention in her mind as she started mentally preparing for the fight.

~*~

Elli dialed her office from her car. "Hey, can I speak to Bob? Sure, I'll hang on."

The hold music played a little loud. She'd have to figure out how to adjust that.

"Yello." Her partner's hello always sounded like he was calling bingo numbers.

"Hey, Bob. Elli, here."

"How's it going at the beach?"

"Good." That wasn't exactly true. "Look, I'm going to being staying down here for a while. Can I get you to cover my clients and any new leads that I get while I'm here?"

"Of course. We can do a split."

"No, I wouldn't expect that. Really if you can just be sure everyone is happy there in Charlotte, I'll be thrilled."

"You got it. Don't worry about things here. You covered me last year when all that was going on."

"Yeah, that's why I feel bad for asking. I know how much work it is, but thanks. I really appreciate it."

"No worries. Just keep me posted on how things are going and let me know if I can help."

"Will do." She hadn't worried even one second that he might not be happy to help, but she did hate asking. It was never something she'd been good at.

With that done she could focus on the problems at hand. Aside from the pier, which there wasn't much she could do until she got all the details at the town hall tonight, she needed to get the beach house ready to show. It'd probably be a lot easier to sell the beach house with Nana out of it. So first things first: Find a house for Nana.

She went straight to Carolina By The Sea so she could use Pam's printer to print out the comps and current listings she'd pulled.

Pam was in the lobby when she walked inside. "Hey there. Just the person I needed to see. Can I borrow an office space for an hour, and I need to ask you about something."

"Sure. Everything okay?"

"I don't know," Elli said.

Pam motioned her to an office next to hers. "You can set up in here."

"Thanks." Elli put her laptop case on the desk and started unpacking the power cable. "I just had the most interesting conversation down at the town municipal center."

"Oh?"

"Did you know there's a chance the pier may not reopen at all?"

Pam sat down in the chair. "I've heard the rumors, but we've heard that before. You don't think they're serious. Do you?"

Elli nodded. "I do. I was just talking to the clerk down there. Evidently there's a big town meeting tonight. I plan on being there."

"Really? I didn't get a notice. Usually all the businesses hear about those meetings. Are you sure it's tonight?"

Elli pulled the flyer from her purse and handed it to Pam.

Pam pressed her lips together. "I'm going to make some phone calls to some of the other small-business owners around. If they are trying to keep it quiet, something has to be up. Make yourself at home here. I'll be there tonight too."

"I was so hoping you would say that. Thanks." She pressed the button on her laptop and the screen lit up. "I won't be long."

"Take your time. And thanks for letting me know about tonight. That's kind of odd."

Once Elli had the listings narrowed down to the ones that met Nana's criteria and had them all charted out in a cohesive route, she tapped on Pam's office door. "Want to ride along to check out some potentials for Nana?"

"Absolutely. I could use a break." Pam grabbed her coat from the rack by the door, and she and Elli headed for the parking lot. "If I know you, you probably have all of this on a precise schedule, but I have a place for you to look at before we get started."

"It's probably on my list."

"No. This one isn't on the market yet. It's my neighbor's house. They're getting a divorce. While you were looking up houses, I took a chance and gave her a call. They are ready to entertain offers. You've got to see it. The place is great. Plus Nana would be right next door to me."

"Great. Let's check it out."

Elli drove toward Pam's house.

"It's the one just past mine."

"Oh, the cute yellow place?"

"Yep. The Lazy Daisy. They own a bunch of florists in Virginia. I love the name."

"Me too." Elli pulled into the driveway. "Nice. Parking for at least four maybe even five cars here."

"Yeah. There's a rental lockout with it too. They never used the place much. Not sure why they've kept it this long."

"Do you have a key?"

"Sure do." She held it up. "I'm their emergency contact."

They got out and walked around the exterior first. "It's in great shape."

"They spent almost a year renovating and remodeling," Pam said. "I think their original plan was to use the rental unit as a potential in-law suite one day."

"I see how they could have made that work. It's great. Lots of light too."

From the ground floor there wasn't much of a view, but the upstairs unit had a clear view of the ocean. "It's gorgeous up here."

"I know. This house sits a little more forward than mine so from this angle it's like you're the only one on the beach."

"Wow."

Pam chattered like an excited squirrel. "I'm thinking the downstairs would be perfect for Nana. Look at all this space. And no stairs. Plus wait until you see the kitchen."

Elli followed Pam into the chef's kitchen. Gorgeous cherry cabinets with green glass fronts picked up the shine in the granite countertops. It was nice to see the rich cherry tones alongside the colors of sea glass. So many people opted for blues and whites that it got old. This seemed fresh and warm. She opened a set of green fogged-glass French doors expecting to go out onto the deck. "It's a pantry. Oh my gosh. Nana would love this."

"And look." Pam walked over to a glassed-in sun porch. "Is this great or what?"

"She could use this as her art studio. Nothing but light. It's perfect."

"I know. And I'd love it with y'all being right next store."

"Y'all?"

"Oh, come on. You should just move back. I miss you like crazy."

"I miss you too."

"There's plenty of room here. You could stay upstairs. Nana isn't getting any younger."

"Don't be putting that guilt trip on me. I could come and visit more often though."

"Okay! That'll work just as well."

Elli walked back upstairs. "I could at least stay up here until Nana gets settled in. Then I could rent it out furnished, and that could cover Nana's bills. It could really work." She could really see the potential. It met all of Nana's criteria too. "Tell them not to list it just yet. Maybe we can bring Nana over here tomorrow to take a look. I have a feeling this is going to be the one, but let's do a ride by on these others on the list…just in case."

"You got it."

Elli drove while Pam called her neighbor, who was almost as excited about Elli's interest as she was. Two of the places were in such poor condition they didn't even bother getting out of the car. The others were okay but couldn't hold a candle to the location of the Lazy Daisy, so they headed back to the spa.

"Thanks for coming with me today. That was fun. Like old times." Elli looked at her watch. "I think I have just enough time to get up to Kill Devil Hills to pick up some tools and supplies for Brody before the town hall meeting. He's going gangbusters on those boards for me. Lot of good that'll be if they shut down the pier though."

"Well, never lose hope. Keep focus on what you want. You get what you expect."

Pam was always finding the positive in every situation. If that girl ever came yelling catastrophe, Elli would be the first one to run because it just wasn't in Pam's nature to worry.

"I'll try. Want me to pick you up for the town hall?"

"No. I'll just meet up with you there." She got out of the car and waved as she went inside the resort to her office.

It would be nice to spend more time here.

CHAPTER NINE

It hadn't been easy finding a parking space at the town hall. Either Pam was just out of the loop about the situation, or she'd hustled up a lot of attention in the past few hours.

Elli's stomach clenched as she got closer to the building. She really hoped this bad feeling in her gut was something she ate and not bad news getting ready to come her way.

Inside, there was standing room only, so she edged her way around the right side and took a spot against the wall. She didn't know as many folks as she used to around here, but she looked for familiar faces and saw a few. She did a double take at the guy sitting all the way across the room. From the back it looked just like Brody.

He was seated next to two men in suits, and it looked like they were having a casual conversation. No surprise. Brody seemed like the type who could get along with anyone.

Then the guy turned and glanced around the room.

It was Brody.

Why would he be here? He must have caught wind about what was going on and decided to come. He probably thought she didn't know. Maybe she should've gone back to the beach house before coming, but she hadn't wanted to lie to Nana and hadn't wanted to worry her either. It had seemed easier just to come straight here. But she could have saved Brody the trip.

Just as the mayor, town council members and committee chairs filed into the room, Elli saw Pam come in. She waved to catch her attention and watched as she excused her way through the crowded room toward her.

"Hey, sorry I'm late, have I missed anything?" Pam said, half-winded.

"No. They're just calling the meeting to order," Elli reassured her.

"Something's fishy. No one I know knew *anything* about this. I went online and it was posted in advance as it's supposed to be, but boy was it hush-hush and buried in the middle of a bunch of other stuff. We rustled up the troops."

"Well, it looks like you did a good job." Elli watched the expression on the faces of the committee members as they took their seats. They didn't look like they'd expected this kind of outpouring. And then she made eye contact with the man sitting to the left of the mayor, and when it all registered, she elbowed Pam so hard that Pam yelped.

"Ow."

Elli whispered through gritted teeth. "Look who is up there."

Pam glanced around, and then her mouth dropped wide open. "I knew he was working for the town, but I had no idea ..."

"I should've known he was up to something when he asked me over and was so nice."

"What?" Pam grabbed her arm. "You went to his house?"

Elli shushed her. "I'll tell you later. It's a long story." A heaviness centered in her chest.

"This is like the craziest day ever."

The secretary got up and read the minutes from the previous meeting.

The facts listed out like that, one by one in a monotone voice, were somewhat depressing and unfortunately accurate.

As the secretary read through the estimates to repair the pier, it became abundantly clear where the meeting was headed. Under the best-case scenario it was a two-year project, and it would cost hundreds of thousands of dollars that the town just didn't have.

Elli wished she could march up there and demand more time to reconsider, but all the Buy A Board campaigns in the world weren't going to raise that kind of money in time to reopen the pier anytime soon. Talk about determining adequate pile bearing capacity, including the static formula method, the dynamic formula method, the wave equation analysis, point bearing piles, and pile load tests made her almost dizzy. Then there were non-water loads, including dead loads, live loads, construction loads, and wind loads to consider. It was an engineering macramé to say the least. On a personal level she was disappointed to the point of sadness, but as a businesswoman she knew that what they were saying made sense.

One by one, locals took their turn at the microphone. Some sad, some angrier than all get-out that the town let this happen. A couple went in for the personal attack on Holden Moore.

Elli had to admit she appreciated those the most.

A guy with a ponytail, wearing a baseball cap with a fish embroidered on the front, stabbed his finger in the air toward Holden as he spoke. "And we brought back a local like you, way overpaid you, to do *this*? What kind of economic development is it to shut down the one real tourism draw we have? You're nuts, man."

Elli wanted to applaud him. Pam did.

The image of that snaggle-toothed jack-o'-lantern popped into her mind. At this point it sounded like there wasn't much anyone could do to revive the pier for this summer any more than they could have revived a rotten pumpkin.

The waitress from the diner who'd been so nice to Holden the other day, Evelyn took the mic next.

"Every one of y'all sitting up there was voted in to help us, or hired in on a platform to save this town's legacy and bring in tourism that would support but not swallow the town. I get it that the insurance and liability of that pier is a problem, but y'all were trying to be all sneaky about this. Don't think we haven't noticed. If I hadn't gotten a well-timed phone call I wouldn't have even known this meeting was going on." She leveled a stare directly at Holden. "And I see some of you several times a week. Not so much as a peep. Seriously?"

Holden spoke into the mic in front of his seat. "The town meeting and announcements made regarding earlier discussions on this subject were made in accordance with the guidelines set for the town of Sand Dollar Cove."

His matter-of-fact tone rubbed Elli like a jellyfish sting.

Apparently the waitress felt the same rub, because she pulled her hands up on her hips. "We don't care if you followed it to the letter. The point is we usually know and we're always here. This was done differently than business-as-usual and I think that's shady. I've said what I have to say."

Someone on the board spoke up. "We realize this isn't what you were hoping to hear tonight, but the truth is that pier has been uninsurable since the storm of 2007. We've done our best to keep it up and going just because of its landmark status, but we have to do what's right for the financial stability of this community. We will be looking into other ways to promote tourism and viable alternatives to facilitate those ideas for our community and the visitors that those pastimes bring to the area."

"Sounds like a political line to me," someone shouted from the crowd.

"Please no comments unless you come to the microphone and state your name."

"Are you going to say anything?" Pam asked.

"What's there to say? It's a budget thing. I can't raise the kind of money it would take to fix it even if they granted it. They've got us over a barrel."

Pam walked over to the microphone and stated her name. "Some individuals have gone the extra mile to raise money to try to fix some of the problems with the pier. Was that even taken into consideration?"

Holden said, "I'll take this one. Yes. Trust me, we are aware of the individual efforts, and we've considered all options, but at the end of the day our mission is to keep this town working toward a long-term plan that will help the town grow."

Pam leaned into the microphone. "And what are we supposed to do with all the materials purchased by people who donated specifically to help this town repair the pier and do just that?"

"That's between the private parties, not a matter for this town council or commission."

"Nice," Pam said, and simply left the microphone.

"Look," Holden said. "Make me the bad guy if you have to, but I love this town as much as anyone. I grew up here, and I wanted to save the pier too. It just isn't in the numbers. Maybe one day it will be, and that can all be revisited. I know lots of you here today participated in the Buy A Board campaign. I'm sorry. My hands are tied. You elected me to help not only keep this town on its feet, but also to expand tourism in a way that fits the community. I'm trying to do that.

"We've sustained considerable damage over the years since then, and the town is simply out of funds to keep it in a safe condition.

"The hurricane took the first two hundred feet. Shortening the pier was an option, but with this last nor'easter taking over two hundred feet from the middle, between pilings, strings and decking, repairs were expected to run over a $1,000 a foot, and that didn't include stabilizing the rest of the structure that was already in disrepair. It's just not safe."

The noise level in the room got louder, and Elli wiggled her way between the bodies and met Pam halfway. "Let's get out of here."

They walked outside. Elli sucked in a lungful of air, and then tears of frustration fell.

"I'm so sorry I didn't know all this was going down."

"It's not your fault. I know what they are saying makes sense in my head, but my heart is so broken. That pier has been a local landmark since the '50s, a part of my family as long as I can remember."

"Well, maybe there's another option. Maybe Nana can put her things in the spa gift shop to sell. Or we find another location or something."

"The only thing I know for sure is that I have piles of lumber that people paid to sponsor already purchased and ready to be personalized. This is one hot mess."

"No one will expect their money back. We can still put those boards to good use in this town somehow. Give us a day or two. We'll come up with something. We always do."

"The guy I brought in to do that work for me, Brody, he was in there. He has got to be wondering what kind of kook I am to drag him all the way out here to work on something that isn't ever going to happen."

"You didn't have any way of knowing, and even if it didn't change the outcome, it was quite clear that this town won't stand for that kind of behavior again."

"At least Brody can start that little vacation he was hoping for early. I sure can't just send him packing because everything just fell apart."

"What was that you were saying about Holden in there?"

"I was hoping you'd forget that."

"And why am I just finding out now?"

"I didn't tell you or Nana because I didn't want y'all to get all crazy-eyed thinking we might get back together or something. Or maybe I didn't want the speech about how I shouldn't go out with him."

"So you really went out with him?"

"Worse. He cooked for me." She closed her eyes. "At his house, and we walked in the moonlight."

"Oh, Elli. No."

"Yes. And we kissed." She felt like such an idiot.

"Come on. This deserves wine. Follow me to my place."

The other night ran through Elli's mind the whole drive over to Pam's. Had Holden just been trying to keep her on his side before things blew up? Why had she trusted him? Or maybe it had been his way of schmoozing her to ease his guilty conscience.

He knew what that pier meant to her...to her family.

He had to have known when he stopped her on the pier the other day. And yet he hadn't said a word. Just let her ramble on about all she had to do. He'd even seen all those stacks of lumber.

Then again, it shouldn't surprise her. It wasn't so unlike that summer years ago. He only told half the truth, and he didn't seem to care if the half he did tell was misconstrued.

But that was water under the bridge, or a dilapidated pier as it were. She ran the back of her hand across her mouth, wishing she'd never given in to his kisses that night. Just one more mistake.

CHAPTER TEN

It was close to eleven when Elli finally got back to the beach house. She'd called and let Nana know she'd be home late so she wouldn't worry, and by the looks of the house she'd chosen to not wait up. The whole house was dark, and that was actually a relief.

She hadn't had the heart to tell Nana what happened over the phone. She was pretty sure Brody wouldn't spill the beans. He didn't seem the type to stir up trouble or invite conflict. She'd have to explain to them both tomorrow.

"We have to stop meeting like this," Brody said.

Elli stumbled backwards, half-startled. "*You* have to quit scaring me to death."

"Sorry. I like it out here."

"Apparently. Have you been sleeping out here too?"

"No, but I would be tempted if it was a little warmer."

"Yeah, it is nice out here." She walked over and stood next to his chair. "So you were there tonight. You know everything I know."

"You didn't see that coming, did you?"

"No," she admitted. Maybe she should have, but even knowing it was a possibility, it had still come as a shock to hear it in certainty.

Brody pushed a hand through his dark hair. "It's a mess. After hearing all the stories about that pier from your grandmother, I have to say it kind of blew me away."

"Well, then you know how I feel." Rather than pull up a chair she sat on the deck cross-legged and set her elbows on her knees. "It's such a mess. I'm sorry I drug you all the way out here for nothing."

"You didn't really. I had other reasons to be out here too."

Probably, finding himself or something simple and uncomplicated like that. Must be nice to be of that mind set. What she'd give for one uncomplicated day like that.

He set his iPad on the table next to him. "Would it make you feel better if I said I think things will improve around here in the future?"

"You psychic or just an optimist?"

His laugh was nice. "Neither. There are always options. So, Elli, what are your options?"

"Bury Holden Moore up to his mouth in the sand and hope the sand fiddlers eat him alive from the inside out?"

"My. You have a little dark side. That was unexpected."

"Sorry. I exaggerate a little when I'm mad." She looked up at the stars. "Maybe I'm more disappointed than mad. And I feel guilty that I haven't been back much to see Nana. I didn't even realize the pier was in that bad of shape. I just whipped up a solution and didn't even consider that things would continue to degrade while I raised money. Plus, I misled all of those people who donated to the project."

"You didn't knowingly do that."

"But that's what has happened. Does it really matter that it wasn't intentional? At the end of the day, it's all the same."

"You'll find another path."

"You were there, Brody. You heard them. Even in the best-case scenario, if I hit the lottery, it's at least a two-year project."

"Never give up hope. You'll think of something. Maybe an interim solution until the pier can be repaired. Keep your mind open. Think outside the box."

She appreciated his optimism, but she was out of energy. "I'm going to call it a night. I hope you know that you're welcome to stay here with us the whole time that we'd planned. It's really the least I could do." She stood.

"Great. I mean, if you don't mind. I'd like to stick around for a while."

She turned to leave and then stopped. "You didn't happen to mention any of this to Nana, did you?"

"No. Not my place. And why don't you wait to say anything to Nana for just a day or two. Let's brainstorm some options first."

"I don't know that there are any, but yeah, let's touch base after I get some rest. Good night, Brody."

CHAPTER ELEVEN

The next morning Elli didn't have any more answers than she had last night. But at least the house stuff was working out. The Lazy Daisy was perfect for Nana, and if Ed fell in love with the Sol~Mate like most everyone who ever visited did, then that would be a done deal.

Elli watched from the deck as Ed Rockingham pulled up in front of the Sol~Mate. He broke into a smile as he got out of his car and took a look around.

"Want to see the beach or the house first?" Elli called out from the deck.

"The house. I love it already." He took the stairs at a quick clip, pushing his sunglasses on top of his head as he hit the top one. "Great place."

"Aren't the views terrific?" She pointed toward the water. "You can see right over the dune line. You'll have uninterrupted views from upstairs. I'll show you, but those dunes are a precious part of the land here. They've kept this place safe from storms for years."

"I like it."

"Wait until you see inside." She opened the front door, and Nana's famous chocolate chip cookies welcomed them. It was the oldest trick in the real estate sales handbook, but it really hadn't been planned. Nana had done that on her own.

Elli led Ed through the first floor, ending in the kitchen where Nana offered him warm cookies.

"Don't mind if I do," Ed said. "Wow, these are really good."

"So, you're thinking of moving here to our little town, are you?"

"Yes, ma'am," he said. "Love your house."

"Thank you. Are you married? Any little ones? It's a lot of house for one. That's the only reason I'm leaving it."

"No wife. Two exes, but I don't see me inviting them over. Especially not at the same time." He laughed. "I do have a son. He'll be twelve this year. I'd love to have a place where he and his cousins could come and spend the summer."

"Oh, that would be great. All of my grandchildren loved staying here. Elli used to spend every summer here. I could even leave the bunk beds for you. I sure don't have any use for them."

"Nana, let me keep showing him around. He hasn't bought the place yet."

"It was nice chatting with you," Ed said as they headed for the stairs.

Nana was standing at the bottom of the stairs when they came back down. "It's a great house. Such a great aura about it. Many, many happy memories here."

Elli had to laugh at Nana's attempt to sell the house. It didn't need any help. It would practically sell itself on location alone. "I'm going to take him down to the beach and show him the rest of the property."

Ed grinned. "It is a great place. I really like it. It's exactly what I had in my head."

Brody walked in the door just as they were heading for it. "Oh, excuse me. Am I interrupting?"

"No," Elli said. "I'm just showing the house. Ed here is looking to relocate to Sand Dollar Cove. Nana and I are going to be putting the Sol~Mate up for sale. He's getting an early peek."

"You're selling?" Brody asked. "Is this ..." He glanced at Nana and back at Elli.

"No. Nana just needs a few less stairs and a lot less space at this stage of her life. We've been talking about it for a while."

"Oh, yeah. Okay. Well, I've only been staying here a few days, but I can tell you this place has a great vibe." He reached for Ed's hand. "Brody Rankin."

"Nice to meet you. Ed. Ed Rockingham."

"I knew you looked familiar. Nice to meet you in person."

Ed seemed casually amused. "Yeah, most people don't put two and two together."

Apparently she was one of those "most people." She'd have to ask Brody about that later. "Shall we?"

"Sure," Ed said. "Nice to meet you, Brody."

Elli kicked off her shoes as they headed for the dunes.

Ed didn't say much as they walked over the dune and down to the beach. She thought he might explain to her his comment to Brody, but since he didn't, she didn't ask.

When they got to the top of the dune, Elli started down and realized Ed had stopped at the top.

He stood there staring out across the wide span of beach. "Wow."

Low tide was always so impressive. Sometimes she took that for granted. She let him take it all in.

Ed took a moment and then headed down to Elli. "I've walked up and down this beach the last week or so. I love it, but nothing is as beautiful as this cove. This is the spot the whole town was named after, isn't it?"

"I like to think so." She walked closer to the where the water was licking the dry sand. "This is how Sand Dollar Cove got its name." She dug her perfectly painted toes into the sand and shifted four small sand dollars to the top. "See."

"No way." He reached down and held them in his hand. "No one comes down to this part of the beach?"

"Not so much anymore. It's private beach now. Part of Sol~Mate."

"I'd own this?"

"Yes, sir. There was a time when you couldn't do what I just did. People were taking the live sand dollars home for souvenirs, and they were diminishing. That's when my great-grandfather built the pier and made this part of the cove restricted. He wanted to let them replenish. Now I think we might have more than we actually need. It's like a sand dollar orgy down here, but Nana comes and gets the retirees and gives them a second life in her artwork."

"Cool. So you just collect some of them? Like a certain size or something?"

"When they die they'll wash up on the shore. We just use those."

"This is amazing. What are all those buildings over there? Some kind of a shopping center?"

"Not anymore. There used to be a bait shack, a little restaurant, and my grandfather made surfboards in the bigger section. It was called the plaza. I don't really know if it ever had an official name, but that's what Pops called it. Matter of fact, my grandmother and grandfather lived in that building while the Sol~Mate was being built."

"Those are with the property too?"

"Yes. The property line goes from over there, where that sand fence is, down to where that light post is then past the plaza. Your own private beach, and there used to be a parking area just beyond there. It was shell sand, still should be a pretty sturdy roadbed there although no one has really used that in years."

Elli started heading up the beach. "Come on. I'll show you around those." She punched in the code and let him in. "My grandfather was using this place as a workshop. You can ignore all the lumber. That's why Brody is here. He's helping me on a project."

"I love the house and the beach. Can't say that I'd need these buildings." But then Ed looked like he had an idea. "Or maybe there is something I could do with them. I'll have to think about that."

Elli hadn't really thought about these buildings sitting out here not being used. Probably because they'd always just been that way. "It's kind of sad how once things finish their time of use they just get let go."

"Sound like that's personal."

"Kind of is. Turns out the pier might not be reopening."

"Not surprised. I saw that big bite out of the middle of it. Made me think of that giant shark in the movie *Jaws*."

"Yeah, last storm that came through did that. Trouble is even though the very front end is fine the town can't afford to make it safe and no one will insure it. It breaks my heart. My Nana has worked that pier for years...as long as I can remember. And I have, or I guess I had, a business there."

"Real estate?"

"No, actually when I was in high school I spent the summers here and my grandfather, Pops, helped me start my very first business to raise money for college. I made homemade ice pops, like Popsicles."

"Enterprising little thing, weren't you?"

"Still am. I select two kids from the local high school each year and let them run the stand. I provide their first supplies and the recipes, then they do the rest. Kind of a scholarship, but a teach-'em-to-fish way of doing it."

"I like that."

"I hate to let that go. Anyway, enough about my problems. What do you think?"

"It's great. Everything I was hoping for. Let me think about it. Would you consider sub-dividing it? I'm not sure I need all of this stuff. Maybe someone else could put it to better use."

"I hadn't really thought about that as an option. I could check." But if Holden was in charge of making those decisions, she didn't hold much hope that his decisions would be in her favor, if yesterday was any indication.

She and Ed walked back over to where he was parked. "Did you want to take a look at those other properties? I've got it all set up."

"You know, I don't think I do. I looked at the others online. They are not even in the same ballpark as this."

He liked the house, and that had been her hope, but now that it actually felt like there was a possibility he'd come back with an offer, an unwelcome feeling of sorrow settled over her. First the pier. Now the beach house.

Nana would be dying to chitchat about every little thing, wanting to know what Ed said. What he liked or didn't. She wasn't up for it. Instead, she headed back over the dune. The beach was a best friend no matter what was going on. And the best part was it never demanded an explanation.

CHAPTER TWELVE

"I thought I might find you here." Brody's voice held its own over the waves breaking. "I brought you something to eat."

Elli let the wet sand run through her fingers and pile upon itself into a stalagmite formation. She was nearly surrounded by the little structures, like her own little fortress. She looked up and met his gaze. "How'd you know to find me here?"

"I'm a beach guy. We beach types...East Coast, West Coast...it's all the same. We aren't all that different. I figured this would be the place you'd come. I mean you seemed so close with your granddad and all. So the beach. Near the workshop. Seemed logical."

"Yeah. Brilliant deduction, Watson...er, Rankin." She laughed at her own joke. "Things are changing so fast."

"The ocean has a way of putting things into perspective, but I have to ask. Why are you sitting in the water in your jeans?"

She'd barely noticed the tide coming up. The water had been a chilly burst when it first slapped against her legs, but she'd gotten used to it, and now, well it probably did look a bit silly to be sitting three feet into the splash zone even if it was only barely over her pant legs. "It was low tide when I got here."

"You've been out here a long time then."

She nodded. The will to get up seemed more than she could manage. She'd prayed that maybe an answer would roll in from the tide. She was plumb out of ideas to save her grandparents' legacy here in Sand Dollar Cove.

"You okay?"

"Just thinking about everything." She lifted a handful of wet sand and wiggled her fingers until just the sand dollars remained. Three teensy ones. She laid the sand dollars on the leg of her jeans. The next wave just washed them back down into the sand.

"With the pier gone," she said, "I hate to think what that town council is going to think is a good next move for Sand Dollar Cove. Some fast food chain setting up shop on one of the main drags? Then what? A mall? A national-chain grocery store? That would be just great. Poor Mr. Martin would never be able to compete against the likes of a Food Lion or Harris Teeter. The locals look out for each other around here. It's simple, and we kind of like it that way. The same families back every year for their annual fishing outings. They'll probably find somewhere else to go."

"Things will change. That's part of the cycle. It's not always bad." He put a hand out to her. "Come on. Let's go sit up on the sand where it's dry and get some food in you."

She reached for his hand, and he tugged her up in one easy pull. Her jeans felt like they weighed about twenty pounds as she trudged up to the dune line. Brody led the way up the beach then plopped down in the sand, and she sat down beside him.

"Here. I made a meatloaf for Nana."

"You really cooked again tonight?"

"I did. Nana said it was the best meatloaf she'd ever had. But I have a feeling she was just trying to work it so I'd cook again."

"She's sly like that."

"I figured sandwiches would be easier on the beach." He handed her one of the paper towel wrapped sandwiches and bit into the other.

"Thanks." She took a bite to be polite, but she wasn't hungry.

"So, I've been thinking," he said.

"Me too. It's a sorry state of affairs."

"You sure got defeated easily."

"It's not like me, but I'll be darned if I can see a way out of this one."

"That's because you're too close to it." He took another bite of his sandwich and let the silence hang between them. "It's why I believe that bringing in fresh members on a team is the best way to problem-solve. Fresh ideas. No connection to what it's always been."

"I'm listening."

"You might have the answer right here. Nana was telling me all about how your granddad's workshop used to be part of the plaza. She also mentioned there'd been some kind of a preservation down here at the cove at one time. Is that still in play?"

"No. It was set for twenty-five years. It can be reopened whenever someone ..." Her eyes widened, and a slight smile played on her lips.

"Like I said. You might be sitting on the answer."

"The plaza?"

"Yeah. I mean it needs work. A lot of work, but it could be done. There's plenty of space. In fact I walked down to the pier. The plaza has more space than the shops on the pier took up. You have room for everything that was on the pier and some new tenants too.

"I can't believe I didn't think of it."

"Because you're too close to it. It's what you've always known it as, just your granddaddy's man cave. But it would be great. With all that lumber you have we could build out something pretty nice. Plus, then technically you're still giving the folks who donated to fix the shops exactly what they paid for."

"Could we get it up by summer?"

"If we do it the old-fashioned way we can."

Something in his manner soothed her. "What exactly is the old-fashioned way?"

"We call in all of our friends. Like a barn-raising."

Elli felt her mood soar. "That's an awesome idea. We could totally do that. We'd need some pretty specific project plans, but this place is solid. Good thing about structures built that long ago, they were built to last."

"You'll have to get the permits, that might take some time, but I think after what went down at the town meeting, they should be in an amicable mood to get the locals back on their side. Those guys I was talking to the other night at the meeting. I think they can help with that."

"Really?"

"Yeah, and this isn't that far off from the pier. I bet if you could get clearance to put some signage down there you could re-route the regulars."

"You're a genius!"

"I'm your genius for the next month or so. What do you say we give this some serious consideration?"

"I say I'm in!"

Elli and Brody raced over to the workshop. It felt good to run off the aggravation that had settled into her muscles. She tugged on her jeans as they slipped low on her hips from the weight of them being so wet.

Brody punched the code into the door lock and then started talking as fast as a seagull going for a French fry. He shared his ideas on how they could build out the space. "The way I figure it, we'll still need the lumber you have, and I took the liberty to write up a preliminary list of supplies." He produced a yellow legal sheet of materials. "It's an informal guesstimate, but I think it's in the ballpark. But for a relatively small investment this can work."

"I've got money I can put into it, and quite frankly Nana will net a pretty big profit off the sale of the beach house. Oh, wait, what am I thinking. If we sell the beach house, this all goes with it."

His brows flickered a little. "Maybe we build out a ground-level place for your grandmother right there. She wouldn't have to move."

"I don't know. I think she's really ready to just downsize, and quite honestly I'm not sure a bunch of construction is healthy to put her through at her age." Then she thought of her talk with Ed. "Unless…you know, when I was talking to Ed he asked about subdividing, but I don't think the town will go for it. Why does everything have to be so complicated?"

"Subdividing and rezoning can take a lot of time," Brody said. "Trust me, if it's one thing I do know it's about how long it takes to get zoning and things like that changed."

"That's not good news."

Brody cocked his head. "Do you think Ed's really interested in the property?"

"He seemed to be."

"Do you have any idea if all of this property is zoned for houses, or if the plaza is still zoned for business?"

"I don't really know. Easy enough to check though."

Brody pulled a tape measure from the workbench. "Help me take a measurement of this place."

The two of them worked their way around the building and got the keys for the other two units from the box hanging on the wall. Brody jotted down measurements in ink on his forearm as they went.

"By the way, how do you know Ed?"

"I don't."

"But you said —"

"Oh yeah, I recognized him. He didn't tell you?"

She shook her head as she backed up for the last measurement.

"He plays guitar. I met him through a friend of a friend once." Then he tugged the measuring tape and it zipped back at him faster than Elli could get there. "You've got about 3,200 square feet of prime real estate here, girl. We could easily turn this into four units, or even make three nice-sized ones and three little kiosk-sized ones at one end."

Elli felt renewed hope. "The kiosk would be perfect for Ever-SOL-Pops. People could walk right up to the window and not track in sand. I like the three and three option."

"I'll work up some drawings."

"You know how to do that?"

"What? Do I just look like another pretty face to you?" he teased.

"No. I didn't mean it like that." But then yeah, she really had meant it that way, and she felt bad for stereotyping him off of just the few conversations they'd had. "Maybe you shouldn't put too much effort into those drawings until we know for sure we can make it happen."

"We're onto something. I have a good feeling about this. If this isn't it, then something else will come up. Besides, you look a lot prettier when you're smiling."

She felt the heat rush in her cheeks. "Thank you." How she got so lucky in finding such willing help through one Facebook post she had no idea.

CHAPTER THIRTEEN

The next morning Elli took Nana to see the Lazy Daisy, and she had the same reaction that Elli had had. It was perfect.

"Let's make a full price offer on it, Elli. I can't wait to get to paint in that sunroom. Maybe I can even do a few canvas paintings again. Do you know how long it has been since I've done anything bigger than a sand dollar?"

Elli had to laugh at that. "No. I guess I never really thought about it."

"Well, probably since you and I made those paintings in your room."

"That *has* been a while."

Nana's blue eyes sparkled. "I think I'll be very happy here. And I can rent out the upstairs. That would be nice. I like having people around."

"And Pam's right next door. I was thinking maybe I'd move down for a few months. Would you mind?"

"Mind? I'd love it!"

"I think that's the plan then. I'll put an offer in on the house, but let me handle the negotiations.

They're going through a nasty divorce. I think we have some wiggle room on price."

Nana grinned. "I'm so proud of you, Elli. Thank you for helping me with this."

Elli appreciated the compliment, but she had to tell Nana about the pier before someone else did. Gosh, this was hard. "Nana, I need to tell you something."

"What is it? You look concerned. You're okay, aren't you?"

"Oh yes, it's nothing like that." But she did feel right sick at the moment. "All that trouble with the license and permit renewal for the shops on the pier ..."

Her smile faded. "They are shutting it down, aren't they?"

"Yes ma'am. They are. I'm so sorry."

"It's okay, Elli. No one can ever take my memories away. That pier has been a real blessing, but it's seen better days. I'm not surprised."

"You're not?"

A soft and loving curve reached her lips. "Of course not. Were you worried I'd be upset about it?"

"Yes. I was. I'm shocked you're not."

"Honey, that pier is a wonderful part of my story, but it's not everything. Every day brings something new. I'm fine with discovering the new things that will become my new memories."

Elli wrapped her arms around Nana. "You're the wisest woman I know. I love you so much."

"And on a bright note, I can slow down on that rampage to get the inventory restocked. I'm about tired of painting seagulls, I can tell you that."

"Well, Brody and I were talking about some other options, so hopefully we'll have a new location for you, but we're going to let that be a surprise."

"I'm sure it will all work out as it should. By the way, someone called and told me they saw you out and about with Holden Moore. Is there a reunion romance brewing?"

"Not at all. Holden is up to the same old games he's always been. He hasn't changed. He has a lot to do with the decision to close the pier. Why can't people just be what they seem? Is that too much to ask?"

"You'll meet someone nice. I'm sure you will, you just have to slow down long enough for someone to catch you. Elli, you have to settle down and just enjoy life at some point. Maybe it will be here. I'd love that. My first great-grandbabies. That would be something pretty special."

"I think I'm going to need a man first. But don't give up hope."

"Oh, you can believe I won't."

Elli had no doubt that was true. "Did you want to take any pictures or measurements before we leave?"

"No. Let's make that offer. There'll be plenty of time for that if it goes through."

"Great." She and Nana piled back into her car.

Bah-duup. Elli picked her phone up from the console and glanced at the message. "Good news. Ed is very interested in Sol~Mate. He just sent a message. He wants to meet me to talk about the house tomorrow. I guess everything really is coming together."

Elli and Nana drove back home, and Elli was just getting ready to head out to Carolina By The Sea, where she could get a decent Internet connection when Brody came up the stairs. "Hey, Brody? Would you mind if I piggyback off of your Internet?"

"Not at all."

"That would be great. I've got to do a couple things and that'll save me a trip down to Pam's."

"Sure. I leave it on. The network is called waves."

"Waves? As in surfing the waves or the Internet, I guess."

"Yeah. Sort of."

"Great. Let me grab my laptop from my car." She ran down the stairs and got her laptop bag out of the car and then came up and turned it on. Brody joined her out on the deck. "You ready?"

"Yep. Got it."

He wrote the password on a piece of paper and handed it to her. Elli glanced at it, and then her fingernails clicked against the keys. "I'm in. Thanks so much."

An hour later she'd made a lowball offer on the Lazy Daisy and they'd already accepted it pending the inspection. No negotiating. It was almost too easy. She pulled together some preliminary paperwork, trying to stay positive about Ed's interest in Nana's house so she'd be ready, and she was already daydreaming about the potential of a new life breathed back into the plaza.

She and Nana ate dinner, and then Nana got to work on her projects while Elli went into the living room to work on a few more things using Brody's Internet access.

"Hey, you," Brody said as he walked into the room.

"Hey."

"You busy?"

"No. Not really. Just catching up on some e-mails. Thanks for letting me hitch a ride on your Wi-Fi. Sure beats trying to do my business from my phone or to keep driving down to the spa."

"No problem. I have something to show you." He waved his tablet in the air.

"Really? Already?"

"May I?" he asked, nodding to the spot next to her on the loveseat.

"Sure." She scooted over, and he slid in and tapped the screen on his tablet, bringing up some drawings. Not just a line sketch either, but like a blueprint with walls and outlets and glass fronts and everything. He even had a 3-D rendering of what the outside would look like with signs hanging in front of each unit.

"Brody. I can't believe this."

He swept his finger and another view displayed. "This would be the side with the smaller shops. Like you said, the Popsicle stand would be great there."

Elli ran her hands across the plans. "Maybe we could do a rotation lease on the other two kiosks, letting local clubs do fundraising in."

"For sure. Or you could do float or bicycle rentals. Something like that where the items could be stored outside."

"That's a great idea!"

"You like it?"

"No. I absolutely love it. The only problem is —"

Brody's brows drew together. "What?"

"I love it so much that I'm going to be really disappointed if the town won't approve this."

He laughed. "Well, I've been doing a little talking to some people I know. You don't know me so you don't have to trust me or take me up on this offer, but I think I can help you. Would you mind kind of letting me take the lead on this part of the project for you?"

She didn't really know what to say. "You know, I can't pay you. I'm just not in a position to …"

"No. I'm not looking for a job or for you to pay me for this. I told you this will be like a good old-fashioned barn-raising. We're talking a community coming together to make something happen."

"And you really think we can do it?"

"Of course." He sat back and leaned in next to her. He popped open another screen. "See this?"

"That's one elaborate spreadsheet." There was a whole lot more to this guy than Boogie boarding!

"This column is the material you already have. Then, over here in this column is the material we'll need. Worst-case scenario, if we can't get some of the things donated, this will be the investment."

"Are you sure? Can I look at that closer?"

"Sure." He handed her the tablet and watched as she studied the numbers and flipped from the spreadsheet to the plans. "This is totally doable."

"I know."

"You have my permission to forge ahead. If we can pull this off, it will be amazing."

He raised his hand and she slapped it in the air. A high-five. She wasn't sure she'd ever really high-fived anyone before. A first for everything.

Elli jumped to her feet, the adrenaline pushing her into a little jig. "I'm so excited."

"I am too. This ought to be a cool project. I'm really glad I ended up here when I did."

"Me too." Emotions tugged at her. Excitement. Gratitude. Attraction. *Keep your mind on the goal, Elli.* "So what do I need to do?"

Brody clicked around on the tablet. "I just sent a project plan to your e-mail address. It's a pretty detailed list, and I've nested the dependent tasks so we can be sure we get things done in the right order. Look it over and tweak as you see fit. Meanwhile, I need you to contact every able body you know who might be willing to hammer, sweep, or even make lemonade. We'll set up a first meeting in front of the plaza as soon as possible."

"I can do that."

Brody stood up. "Well, then I think we just started."

She could barely contain her excitement. "Yes!" A little squeal escaped, and she knew she had to look like a silly schoolgirl, which should be no surprise because she suddenly felt like one. "I'm sorry. This is just better than I'd ever imagined." She reached up and hugged him. "Thank you so much. You're the best thing that could have happened to me right now."

CHAPTER FOURTEEN

Elli worked into the wee hours of the morning putting together a flyer and a list of e-mail addresses for everyone she knew who might be able to come and help them rebuild the plaza. Even her friends from Virginia. Then she drafted the blast e-mail. If Brody could make this happen, she was going to be ready to roll.

Exhausted, she slid between the sheets, but she could hardly sleep with all the possibilities racing through her mind. After two hours of tossing and turning and looking at the clock she gave in, got up and headed downstairs to make some coffee.

Brody must not have been able to sleep either because when she got downstairs, he'd already made a pot and was sitting at the kitchen table with his tablet working on something.

"Good morning, sunshine," he said.

"You made coffee. Thanks." She poured a mug and joined him at the table.

"Did you by chance pull the plat on the property to see how things are zoned?"

She nodded. "Sure did. The plaza is still zoned business. It's all tied into the same deed, but it's two lots."

"Perfect. I was e-mailing with my guy last night. That's exactly what we needed to hear."

"How soon can we get all hands on deck?"

"I drafted my e-mail and made flyers last night. I'm ready to give it a try whenever you are," Elli said.

"We'll need some time to get the permits. I'll handle that," Brody said. "Let's shoot for April 1ˢᵗ."

"Let's make it the second. We don't need any April Fool's surprises."

"Superstitious?" Brody seemed amused.

"Cautious."

Nana walked in and pulled her hands up on her hips. "What are you two up to before the crack of dawn? Or have you even been to bed yet?"

"I just got up." Elli and Brody exchanged a smile. "But we are working on something very exciting."

Brody got up. "I'll let you fill her in. I'm going to jump in the shower and go down to the plaza and go through the list of materials."

"The plaza?" Nana raised a brow. "Now what exactly are you two up to?"

Elli got up and poured Nana a cup of coffee. "Sit down. You're going to love this."

~*~

On April 2nd cars filled the old plaza parking lot and lined up down the road that led to Sol~Mate. Brody had spearheaded all the permit stuff. People had come out in full force to help with the project to renovate the plaza.

After sending out e-mails to everyone she knew, near or far, Elli had spent the better part of the day yesterday stopping in at every local business to hand out flyers and ask for help. At Brody's suggestion she cruised to where the new houses were being built in the neighboring town and told the guys on those construction sites about it too.

There were twice as many people here than she'd touched base with. Everyone seemed to have brought their handiest or willing friends along to help. And unlike the crowd at the town hall, everyone here was smiling and jovial. Elli wondered how often this type of gathering occurred anymore.

Even if they failed, she felt like a part of something overwhelmingly special just to have even gotten this far.

Nana passed around her famous cookies and thanked everyone personally for coming out.

At six o'clock on the dot, Brody stood up on a chair and whistled to get everyone's attention. "Listen up. Thanks for coming out today. You've all heard that we want to revitalize this old plaza to house the old shops on the pier along with a couple new businesses. I think we have a viable solution to the pier closing that will satisfy the locals and help your community continue to attract new tourists too."

Someone in the crowd gave a whoop!

"Funding is tight, and so is our timeline, so we want to make this happen as quickly and seamlessly as possible. Elli, you want to fill them in?"

"Sure. First of all, thank you from the bottom of my heart. Those of you who know the Eversol family and me know that Sand Dollar Cove is really special to us. My grandmother and grandfather met and fell in love on that pier, and they've run those shops for over forty years. It's common knowledge now that the pier is not going to reopen."

A few people starting chatting amongst themselves. She didn't want to lose their attention so she forged ahead.

"It's okay. As time moves on, sometimes things have to change too. We can make this change for the better. I'm so thankful you're willing to donate your time to help make this a reality."

One glance at Nana's beaming face and Elli felt tears of appreciation tickle her nose. She swept them away. "We're going to revitalize this old plaza. It's been over forty years since it operated down here on the cove. My granddaddy used it as a workshop, and for the past five years it's pretty much just collected dust...but we can do this. We want to do this like a barn-raising. All hands on deck. And quickly. We can keep the costs down that way and ensure we can open with the beginning of the season. Who's in?"

Everyone cheered.

"We can do it," said a guy in a blue ball cap and khakis.

"I was on a Habitat for Humanity team once. In one weekend we built a whole house from nothing to done, and that included finishing work and stuff. All we need is the shells of the storefronts to get you past the inspection. Totally doable."

One man raised a hand in the air and said, "I can do the electrical. I'm certified to do that work in this town."

Brody stepped forward. "Excellent. That's an important point to make. We do want to make fast progress, but we want to do it right the first time. I need everyone to let me know your area of expertise and availability. We'll align you to the tasks so we don't waste anyone's time or talent. Don't worry if you don't have any skills...we need people cleaning up, fetching, and just keeping everyone fed and hydrated too. There's something for everyone to do."

"This is going to be fun."

"It's great."

Elli beamed. Brody pointed to a guy in a black polo shirt standing in front of a card table. "Anyone willing to commit to a time slot and tasks please talk to my buddy, Kenny, over there. He's the man with the plan."

Almost the entire crowd moved at one time.

Elli turned to Brody with so much joy in her heart she felt a bottomless satisfaction. "We're going to really do this!"

He took her two hands into his. "Yes ma'am. We sure are."

"How do you know all of this stuff?"

Brody smiled, but this time there was a hint of sadness in his eyes. "My dad was a contractor. He could build anything. I had the coolest tree fort in the state of California. I worked by his side for years."

"Why don't y'all work together anymore?"

"I haven't worked with him for a while. I found my own niche and moved on. Dad died unexpectedly last year. It's been kind of a hard year."

"I'm so sorry."

"Thank you. Not sorrier than me. I'd been so busy I'd barely seen him that last year. I never thought in a million years he'd die so young. I wasted valuable time."

"Hindsight is always so clear. I'm sorry for your loss, and the timing of it, but I thank you so much for being here for my family."

"This is as much for my dad as it is for your Nana."

"Best motivation ever," Elli said. Being back in Sand Dollar Cove felt so right. "Oh, and I'm meeting Ed tomorrow to discuss the house. Keep your fingers crossed."

Brody crossed his fingers. "It's going to be hard to hammer like this, you know."

"Somehow I'm sure you'll find a way."

~*~

Elli got up and dressed, but Brody had already headed out. The first of the work teams should be on site already, and Brody and Kenny were working from the detailed plan that would keep everything on track. She resisted the temptation to stop in and check on things, trying to give Brody the respect and trust he deserved for taking on such a huge project, but she still slowed down and ogled the work that was already getting underway as she drove by. A half-dozen trucks spotted the parking lot, and someone had pulled a big flatbed trailer in front of the plaza. It looked like they were already clearing the space.

She sang to the radio all the way to Carolina By The Sea. Aside from some spa guests, Elli seemed to be one of the first regular customers at the restaurant this morning. While she waited for Ed, she reviewed the updated paperwork Brody had left for her. Since the last version she'd seen, there were now even more detailed tasks with names aligned to them and even a timeline with a detailed materials breakdown for each phase.

If all went according to plan, the major part of the renovation would be done in seventy-two hours, and they'd be all done except the paint on the walls. All said and done, in ten days it would be complete right down to hanging the sign over the door.

"Hi, Elli. Am I interrupting? You kind of look like you're in deep thought."

"Hi, Ed. No, please join me. I was just looking over some paperwork for something else while I waited for you. Well, yes, I guess I was kind of in deep thought, but sit. Please."

"Something wrong?"

"No. Not really, in fact things are good. It's business."

"I happen to be a pretty good businessman, and a great listener. Try me."

She quickly brought him up to date on what had happened since she'd seen him last. "Now I just have to figure out the best way to fund all of this without going broke. A lot of my assets are tied up. But that's not your problem. So, I hope you're still interested in the house and not the plaza. I realize that changes the deal we originally discussed when I showed you around."

"That works fine. The plaza could really add to the town's revenue in the long haul too. And there's still enough privacy beyond those dunes that the beach house won't be impacted at all. How much do you need?"

"I've worked up a new asking price for just the beach house. And here's the plat too." She pushed the information across the table.

"Seems fair, but I meant how much capital do you need to raise for your project?"

"Oh, Ed, I wasn't hinting at a donation."

"I'm not offering to give you any of my money."

"Oh." She wished she could slurp back the comment because now she felt really silly.

"But I can help you raise the money."

He had her attention. "How would you do that?"

"I'll play a benefit concert for you."

She wasn't quite sure how to tell him thanks but no thanks. It wasn't likely they'd raise much money playing music in a town the size of Sand Dollar Cove. But Brody had said Ed played guitar. To be polite she said, "What kind of concert?"

He reached into his pants pocket and pulled out his phone. "Here. I guess Brody didn't tell you."

"Tell me what?"

"I just assumed when he recognized me the other day that he told you. Here." Ed started a video on his phone and turned it toward her.

"You're going to get Cal Blackwood to play a concert here?" *I don't think that's going to happen?*

"I stand next to him over two hundred nights a year." Ed laughed. "And that's me." He pointed to the screen. "Last week. In front of 50,000 people."

"What?" She grabbed the phone from his hand. "That's you? That IS you. Wow, how do you play while you're spinning around like that?"

He gave her a rock star smile.

"How did we not know?"

"I don't usually tell people. I mean Cal can hardly go anywhere without someone recognizing him, but I can. And I just want to have a quiet place on the beach. Touring is a blast. I love the music, but I need to spend less time on the road and more time in a home I can call my own. A place I can spend time with my kid and just enjoy the simple stuff."

"This is the perfect place to do that. But if you help me by playing a concert, you'd be sacrificing your anonymity. I can't let you do that."

"If I'm going to live here, I want to be a part of the community. I'm sure people will respect that. I have a good feeling about this place. If I'm wrong, well, then better to find that out now."

"You'd do that for me?"

"Yeah. I would." Then he grinned. "Besides, those shops are going to improve the value of my beach house. Don't you go raising the price on me. In fact, don't show it to anyone else. That's why I was tracking you down. I've already spoken to my agent. He's moving funds around right now."

"You're kidding me?"

"Nope."

She reached out and shook his hand. "Welcome to Sand Dollar Cove, neighbor. Now let's talk about that concert."

CHAPTER FIFTEEN

For sixty hours straight, people came and went, and the progress on the plaza was like watching one of those time-lapse videos. Walls were built, plumbing corrected and new wiring pulled just to ensure there wouldn't be any fire hazard down the road.

The local heat and air conditioning company donated a used unit and was scheduled to install it in the morning. The miracles Brody were pulling off just kept besting themselves.

Nana set up a makeshift sweet tea stand and was doling out encouragement like smiles on Sundays. Elli carried a big cup full of iced sweet tea with her for Brody. She wasn't sure if he'd even slept the last two days.

"You need to take a break," she said handing him the cup.

"Thanks for bringing this." He took the lid off and gulped half of it down. "Things are moving right along. We've bumped into a few snags, but nothing we couldn't fix pretty quickly with the right guys on site. What do you think?"

"It's nothing short of a miracle."

"I had an idea I wanted to run past you. What do you think about revitalizing that skimboard stuff your grandfather used to do? I was thinking maybe I could sponsor a skimboarding contest. The first annual one this year. It could draw some folks in. We could plan it for July."

"I love the idea. I wonder what kind of insurance you'd need for an event like that?"

"I don't know, but I have someone I can ask to look into it and start working up some details. I wanted to float it past you first."

"I think it's an awesome idea."

"You still owe me some skimboarding time together. How about later tonight? Under the moonlight?"

"Sure. You're on. There's a full moon tonight. It'll be perfect."

A smile tugged at the corner of his mouth. "I was thinking exactly the same thing. Oh, and I forgot to tell you that the inspector came about an hour ago to check the plumbing and electrical."

"Do I want to hear this?"

"We're in good shape. Now we just have the final inspection to go. One last hurdle." When he smiled, his eyes danced, and that made her insides dance a little too. "I have something for you. Wait right here."

She stood her ground as he disappeared inside the building.

When he walked back out he was carrying the SandD's Gift Shop sign. Repaired and brightly painted. "Brody! It's perfect."

"Think she'll like it?"

"Yes. Absolutely."

"Good." He set it down in front of the corner storefront. "It'll look good." He clapped his hands together. "So we're getting down to the details. By tomorrow, we'll be able to let the teams go. All we'll be doing is waiting on the drywall to cure so we can start priming and painting. I rented a dehumidifier to help speed that along. If it rains that could slow down the drying time, but we're right on schedule."

"We can do that ourselves. I love to paint."

"Great. If we do the cut-in overnight, I can get the guys to finish it the following day. Then all that's left is the final inspection."

"Perfect. I'll be your overnight date tomorrow night," she said, and she liked the way his eyebrows perked when she said that.

"But tonight you're my skimboarding date."

"Yep. How about you come up for dinner and then we'll head out."

"You're on. I put the skimboards in the back storage area. Want me to just grab two?"

"Oh no. You pick one out for yourself. I have a special one."

"Have I met my match?"

"Wait and see."

~*~

"I was beginning to think I'd been stood up," Elli teased when Brody finally came inside for dinner.

"Not on your life. Do I have time to take a quick shower?"

"Take your time."

He whistled softly as he climbed the stairs.
When Elli heard the shower start running, she
turned and caught Nana staring at her with her
dimples so deep it looked almost like someone had
reached up and squeezed her cheeks.

"I know what you're thinking."

"Me?" Nana chuckled and moved along. "No
need for me to put words to it, honey. It's all in the
air. I'm headed to my room."

"You're not going to eat with us tonight?"

"No way." Nana grabbed a jar of peanut
butter and a sleeve of Ritz crackers and marched
out of the room. "I'll be upstairs."

Elli went over to the stove, cranked up the
temperature on the crab pot and sprinkled a healthy
dose of Old Bay seasoning into it. Then she cracked
open a beer took a generous sip and dumped the
rest into the water.

Once she heard the shower turn off, she took
the salads out of the refrigerator and put them on
the table, and then dropped the shrimp into the pot.
Boiled shrimp was about the only thing she could
cook and guarantee success.

She was just pulling the last of the jumbo
shrimp out when Brody walked in wearing a pair of
flowered boarding shorts and a T-shirt. With his
hair wet he looked like he could be on the cover of
one of those fitness magazines, and it was all she
could do to peel her eyes off of him.

"Smells great."

"It should be. Sit down."

They ate, and then Brody helped Elli clear the
table and wash the dishes. "I think our forty-five

minutes between eating and playing in the water is up. You ready to hit the beach?"

"Oh yeah. I've been waiting all day for this. And in case you didn't know, there's nothing better than the cove on a full moon."

"I'll be the judge of that." He took her hand, and she was surprised by the gentleness of his touch. "Let's go."

He led the way outside, and when they hit the last step of the stairs, she veered off to the right and picked up a bright pink skimboard.

"Oh, I see you've already chosen your weapon. Didn't see that one down in the shop."

"I might have had this one stored here," she said with a raise of her brow. "Don't tell me you didn't spend some time picking the perfect one out."

"You're right. I did survey them pretty closely. I left mine down on the other side of the dune. You seem to be ready for a little competition."

"Oh you better believe it."

"First one to hit the water gets the first point." He took off running.

She shouted after him. "Think you need a head start?" She was laughing as she ran, but he wasn't running too hard because she caught up to him fairly easily.

The moon glowed on the water.

By the time they hit the beach they were both laughing. He snagged his board on the run down, but Elli beat him to the water. She tossed her board ahead of her and ran right up behind and leapt on top of it fully clothed, skimming for a good fifteen feet before she hopped off. It was just like riding a bike.

Brody yelled, "Nice." Then he hit the water just as a wave broke and rode it in, lifting the board in a hop and turn until he was almost right in front of her. "You do know what you are doing, girl."

"Can't take the beach out of the girl." She carried her board just above where the waves were coming in and quickly wiggled out of her jeans. They were already wet, but it was hard to skimboard in jeans, and she had her bathing suit on underneath. Then she picked up her board and took off again in the other direction, this time leaping onto the board in a squat and then turning around in a spin as she glided along the moon-swept water.

It didn't take long for Elli to realize Brody might have been sandbagging with just how good of a skimmer he was, because she'd about exhausted her talents when he started flipping his board in the air and riding the waves a little farther out to where they'd crested.

Out of breath, she took her board up and sat on it and watched him. "You rock, man!"

He played to her applause for another good ten minutes before he finally came up and dropped his board next to hers. "I've never ridden one of these old boards before. Your old gramps knew what he was doing."

"He taught me how to skimboard before I even knew how to swim."

"I bet those are some good memories."

"Oh yeah. It's been a long time since I've done that. I have a feeling I'm going to be sore tomorrow." Elli rubbed her hands along the sides of her legs.

"Worry about that tomorrow. Tonight, there's a full moon and this is great." He grabbed her hand and lay back in the sand.

She followed his lead. The sky was full of stars, but they paled in comparison with the bright moon.

Brody rolled over on his side and propped himself up on his elbow. "Isn't it neat the way the moon seems to lay a path through the water?"

"Yeah. The water's choppy tonight, but on a still night it looks like you could walk on it."

"You are full of surprises, Elli Eversol."

"So are you."

He leaned in.

When she'd first seen him she'd found him handsome in an outdoorsy, rugged sort of way, but tonight...he was disturbingly handsome with the moon making his skin shine.

Her hand slid down his arm, sweeping the water droplets from his skin. She could almost feel his thoughts.

His gaze focused on her lips and she wished he would just kiss her already. A sense of tingling anticipation swept through her.

A sensuous smile came to his lips, and then his mouth covered hers, brushing hers in a tantalizing invitation for more as he settled his hand on her hip.

All of the air expelled from her lungs in one wild gasp.

He planted taunting little kisses along her lips, her cheek, and then ever so softly to the crook of her neck. And those sent shimmers as bright as the stars coursing through her.

"I really like who you are, Elli Eversol." He whispered into her ear. Then he straightened and gazed into her eyes.

Elli could feel the heat from his body so close to hers.

He leaned forward and dropped another kiss to her lips, then her nose, and then her forehead. "When I responded to your note on Facebook, this was the last thing I ever expected."

"You're just impressed by my skimboarding skills," she teased, because if she didn't she was liable to let this go a whole lot further than a first kiss should ever go.

"Oh, yeah. And so much more." He sat up. "You ready to call it a night?"

She wasn't. She had a million naughty thoughts running through her mind right now, but she sat up and let him help her up instead. They walked hand in hand over the dune and set their boards next to the house to dry.

His hand settled on the small of her back as they took the stairs up to the deck.

She paused at the front door. "I had the best time tonight."

"You're not the only one." He glanced over his shoulder. "I'm going to sit out here for a while before turning in. Good night." He kissed her on the neck. "I hope you have sweet dreams."

She smiled and went inside, wishing with every step that the door might open behind her and he might follow her to her room.

~*~

Brody had already left for the plaza when Elli woke up the next morning, but rather than check in on him she chose to spend the day with Nana instead.

She had a painting date with Brody tonight, and a little space between last night under the moon and tonight would probably keep some perspective on the situation, although *giddy* was about the best way she could describe what she was feeling for him right now.

At the end of the day she walked down to the plaza. Brody was shaking hands and thanking the last of the workers when she showed up ready to help with the painting.

Wearing an old pair of sweatpants and a T-shirt that had seen better days, she couldn't be accused of trying to impress him. "Ready?" she asked.

Brody turned and gave her a once up and down. "Looks like you are."

She gave him a dramatic curtsey. "New fashion statement."

"Shabby chic. You look adorable, let's see how good you paint."

"Even better than I skimboard. You're on."

He poured paint into two trays, and the two of them got right down to work.

They knocked out the three small kiosk-sized spaces first. "These look incredible," Elli said. "I wish we'd thought to do this years ago."

"It's turned out really nice. I'm glad you're happy with it."

"I'm thrilled." She turned to face him. "Thank you so much for everything. I don't know how things would have played out if you hadn't happened on my path."

They worked for two more hours, making short work of painting out the space.

Finally, they completed the task.

"I can't believe this has come together after it looked like everything was falling apart," she said, stepping back to admire the shop.

"Sometimes good things fall apart so that better things can come together."

"Like this."

"Like us." He reached for her hands, only she was still holding her paintbrush.

She grimaced. "Sorry."

He started laughing. A true from-the-soul laugh. "No. It's perfect. I think it's a sign."

"A sign? I'm not sure a handful of wet paint is a good sign."

He held his hand out and shook his head. "Now that's a matter of perspective. You see," he said stepping closer to her, "they say love…real love…is messy." He swept his finger across her nose and then across her lips. "Maybe we're on the path to something very special."

"You did not just do that."

"Yeah. I think I did."

"Is this the adult version of pulling pigtails?"

"You'd look totally hot in some pigtails."

She raised the paintbrush in her hand.

"You wouldn't," he said.

"Wouldn't I?" She took a step forward to match his step back. "Come here, superhero. Let me put a big S on your chest."

"Only if you'll let me put a kiss on those lips."

This was totally unexpected, but in an amazingly great way. She'd felt something, a spark, but was trying to convince herself that he'd been such a help at just the right time that it was appreciation, not something bigger. But maybe it was. Last night couldn't have been better if they'd planned it, but the fact that it hadn't been planned made it all that more special. It had been spontaneous and easy.

She wiggled her shoulders and took another step toward him with the paintbrush high in the air like a torch lighting her way, a nervous giggle taunting him as she moved closer.

He stood his ground. Tempting her to come forward.

She took the next step, but in one motion he swept her off her feet into his arms. He'd moved so fast, the paintbrush fell from her hand. "Now what, Missy?"

"No S?"

He put her down but didn't release her. Instead he pulled her into his arms and kissed her. And this kiss swept her away like the biggest wave as the tide shifts, tugging you out in a riptide...a little helpless and yet a thrilling yet dangerous ride you can never forget.

Then he pulled her hand in his, wet paint and all, and traced an S on her shirt with his finger.

"I was going to do that to you."

"S for special." He laced his fingers between hers. "I just want to hold your hand and sit here taking in this moment."

"I might just let you, because I'm not sure what could make tonight any more special."

"I think we're ready for the final inspection now," he said.

Oh, she was ready for so much more.

~*~

The next morning Elli went down the final list for the inspection and realized she'd forgotten to pick up the fire extinguishers from the hardware store. She couldn't take a chance on the inspector coming first thing in the morning and not having them, so she texted Pam.

Elli: I know it's the crack of dawn. I need to borrow something. You up?

Pam: I am now. What time is it?

Elli: 6

Pam: Ugh

Elli: I need to borrow two fire extinguishers. I forgot to pick mine up from the hardware store and the inspection is this morning.

Pam: Meet me. Spa. 7.

Elli: You're not going to believe my night.

Pam: Tell!

Elli: See you at 7.

Pam: That's not fair. Make it 6:45.

Elli knew that would get Pam's night-owl butt out of bed. She did love good gossip, and she was a hopeless romantic. If anyone would appreciate what was going on between her and Brody, it would be Pam.

She jumped in the shower and got dressed, but with still plenty of time to spare she couldn't just sit here waiting. She was too nervous and excited about the inspection...not to mention last night. She couldn't wait to tell Pam about Brody. He wasn't at all who she'd have pictured as her own Mr. Perfect, but he made her feel everything she'd never felt before. And that felt right.

Elli got in her car and drove down to the spa. The restaurant opened at six so she'd grab a cup of coffee and wait for Pam there.

"Just one?" the host asked.

"Yes, please. And I'm meeting Pam. If you can just let her know I'm in here when she gets in that would be great."

"Yes, ma'am."

But that *ma'am* thing sure took the sizzle out of that eye candy in a hurry. Polite was great, but if she felt old she could imagine how the older ladies felt. She followed the young man to a small two-topper near the windows. "Thank you."

"You're welcome. Alex will be your waiter, but can I get you some coffee for now?"

"Yes, thank you." She turned her cup over on the table, and he was at her side in an instant with the carafe.

"I'll just leave this for you."

"That'll be perfect." She might even forgive him for calling her ma'am for leaving the whole pot of coffee. She didn't know why she was so nervous about today's inspection. Just one last hurdle. They'd gotten so much done, and quite frankly even if the inspection didn't pass they had plenty of time to get everything done and still be on schedule for an on-time season launch. Things were fine. More than fine, really.

Brody had made her feel so alive. The plaza project, and last night was unexpected and perfect.

"Excuse me. How are you doing?"

She looked up and her mood sank. "I'm fine, Holden."

"Can I sit down?"

She didn't see why she should let him. Maybe if she took long enough to answer he'd just move on.

"I'll just be a moment," he said as he slid into the seat across from her.

So much for that strategy.

"I thought we had a good time that night over dinner."

Was he actually going there? She never was good at hiding her feelings, so she could just imagine the look on her face right now. "You mean the perfect pull-out-every-romantic-trick-in-the-book dinner the night before you ruined everything I've known in Sand Dollar Cove? That night?"

"It wasn't personal, Elli."

"Wasn't it?"

"No. I was hired to do a job. That was not an easy decision."

"And if it was such a business-focused decision why didn't you tell me? It wasn't like you didn't have time. You could have said something the day you carried the SandD's Gift shop sign for me. Over dinner. On the beach."

"I didn't want to ruin a perfect night. I told you that I'd missed you."

"I remember. I was there." But she sure wished she wasn't here right now.

"Can't you at least let me explain?"

She folded her arms across her chest. "Go on."

"Coming back to head up the commission for economic development seemed like a no-brainer for a local like me. I was ready to come home and be closer to my parents, and I'd kind of hoped you'd still be around."

"I really find that hard to believe."

"Elli, I know the old pier is legacy here in Sand Dollar Cove. It's special to a lot of people, not just you. It wasn't an easy choice."

"You made it look effortless."

"It wasn't, and quite honestly, it's all worked out even better for the shops. The plaza, that place is going to be perfect. Everyone is talking about it."

"No thanks to you."

"So, what? You can forgive Brody Rankin for swooping in and saving the day so he can schmooze in a few points with the locals before his company moves to town. I heard he pitched an annual skimboarding competition. I'm sure he wants to do it down at the cove."

Her heart lurched to a stop. So what? "Wait. What did you say about Brody?" She sat forward. "No. Never mind. You leave Brody out of this conversation."

Holden leaned back in his chair. "Oh. I get it now. You like him."

"That is none of your business."

"Amazing. Going for the rich guy. Guess I hadn't made it big enough for you. I kind of thought the house would've impressed you. But I can't compete with a corporate jet and a multimillion-dollar company."

Elli felt like she was in the middle of a pinball game and Holden was just beating the flappers senseless. "I have no idea what you are talking about."

"Wait. Really? You don't know that he owns R waveSTYLE, and that they're closing a deal right now to build an East Coast distribution center out in the new industrial park here in town?"

Her mouth was moving, but nothing was coming out. Why wouldn't Brody have told her about that? Holden had to be mistaken. Brody wasn't...but then what did she really know about him, except that his dad had died. They used to work construction. She knew a lot about his past, not so much about the now, except for the part where he'd swept her off her feet. "Are you sure we're talking about the same person?"

"Google him. Good luck with that." He'd practically barked the words at her. Her mind was tossing possibilities around, and nothing was making sense. She pulled her phone out of her purse and opened the browser.

Brody Rankin.

She clicked on images. There he was. A page of pictures of him. In a suit. At charity events. Riding the waves. With beautiful women right and left. Most eligible bachelor. Shirtless on the beach. In front of R waveSTYLE.

"Hey girl!" Pam tapped her wrist. "Right on time. Are you impressed?" She slid into the chair that Holden had just abandoned.

Elli swallowed, trying to shake the thoughts from her head and push them aside. She had things to do. Important things. "Yeah. Good."

"What's wrong with you? You're acting like someone slipped a mickey in your coffee or something."

"Yeah. I kind of feel like that." She wiped her hand across her forehead.

Pam looked worried. "Are you serious? Are you okay?"

"No. Yes. I'm fine. No one drugged me."

"Get up. Come on, let's have coffee in my office." Pam waved one of the waiters over to help them. "Bring some coffee and ice water to my office, would you?"

"Yes, ma'am."

Elli and Pam walked back out front and down the hall to her office. "What's going on? You sounded fine when you texted me less than an hour ago."

"Holden stopped by while I was waiting on you."

"That jerk. He's not trying to mess up the stuff with the plaza, is he? Because I'll call —"

"No. No, he actually wished me well. Said the whole pier thing wasn't personal."

"Whatever. Don't let him ruin your day. Everything is going your way. And tell me about your night."

Elli leaned forward with her elbows on her knees and covered her eyes. "Why am I such a fool when it comes to relationships?"

"I'm sorry. I'm just not following you." Pam picked up a glass of water. "Here, take a sip."

"I had the most amazing night with Brody last night. He made me feel things that I have *never* felt before. I mean, like seriously, never."

"That's good. Right?"

"Just the touch of his hand on mine. Skimboarding in the moonlight. Silly, stupid stuff. He put paint on my nose. It seemed perfect. So, perfect. And yet he's not the kind of guy I'd have ever even considered going out with."

"That's okay. Sometimes we don't know what we want until we find it. Sounds like you found it, so why are we so upset?"

"Holden said that Brody is really here in town because his company is getting ready to open a big East Coast distribution center here."

"He's R waveStyle?"

"You know about that?"

"Sure. It's been all the talk. I mean I don't think it's been announced that it's a sure thing, but folks are hopeful. It'll bring great things to our region."

"Then why didn't he tell me?"

"You'll have to ask him that."

"Why bother? I can't be with someone who would lie or mislead me. It's Holden all over again."

"Now wait a minute, Elli. I understand this catches you off guard, but he didn't lie. He's a rich, successful guy, but you fell in love with who he is, not what he does for a living."

"I thought he was just some surfer guy with a super big heart."

"And he probably is. The fact that he came in by charter instead of on a bus didn't tip you off just a little? I mean, even I thought that was a little weird."

"I guess I didn't really think about that."

"Don't let Holden mess this up for you too. I've never seen you happier than what you've been since Brody hit town. Plus, Nana adores him. That has to be good for something. She has a great intuition about people. She never did like Holden, if you remember."

"True. Well, I guess I better just get through this inspection. Heck, he'll be gone anyway. You should see all the stuff online about him. He's not going to settle in Sand Dollar Cove or with a simple girl like me."

"I'm sorry, Elli. I really am."

"Me too. I've got to go."

"Hang on." Pam pressed the speaker button on her phone.

"Yes, ma'am."

"Can you get someone to take two fire extinguishers out to the car in the visitor spot right next to mine?"

"On it," the voice came back over the speaker.

"Okay, so that'll just take a moment. But get your head back on straight here before you leave. Y'all have done an amazing thing down there. You're a good team. You got a whole building renovated in less time than it took me to just paint. Where was he when I was starting my project?"

"Guess he couldn't use your land to have his big annual skimboarding competition."

"You don't really think he needed to manipulate you for that, do you?"

"I really don't know what to believe. I thought I'd found him on Facebook. Totally random. It feels very set up now."

"You look beat."

"I am, but I'll be okay." Elli got up and took her keys out.

"Just promise me you'll slow down and listen to all the facts before you do anything crazy."

~*~

It wasn't fifteen minutes after Elli hung the fire extinguishers on the hooks installed for them that the inspector walked in.

The man had to be close to retirement age. His blue Dockers and white shirt were starched stiff, and his tie was a little too short for a man of his height. One of her pet peeves.

"Good morning. I'm so glad you could get here so early. I'm excited to get this last inspection done and start moving forward."

"I'm sure you are. You sure did slap this up in a hurry."

"Well, we had a lot of hands and man hours. If we stretched that out to work days by spreading the allocated time over —"

The inspector held up his hand.

"Too much?"

"Yeah. It was just a comment. I wasn't asking for a math word problem." He started walking through the space, marking on his clipboard.

She didn't mean to upset him. "I can assure you we took every precaution to be sure we stuck to code and did things right. It was a true team effort. Kind of like an Amish barn-raising." Her heart two-stepped, thinking about the first time Brody had compared their project to that. It had seemed so special.

"This isn't a barn," the inspector said matter-of-factly.

"No, but if a town can build a barn from scratch, why not a small set of shops where there was already a foundation?"

"When was this space last used?"

"Years ago."

"I see all the wiring was upgraded. Nice work."

Thank goodness Brody had decided to upgrade those things as they went along. The price now was way less than a repair later.

The man scribbled on that clipboard like a madman. The pen made loud tap and scratch sounds as he did and that was rattling her.

The more he wrote, the more she felt like she might just faint from the anticipation of it all. "Can I get you some coffee? Sweet tea?"

"Won't be here that long," he said, never taking his eye off the outlets.

Elli quit puppy-dogging him around. She wasn't helping. Plus her knees felt like they wouldn't hold her much longer. She probably should have eaten something this morning.

"Well." He walked back toward her, still writing something and then fumbling with some pages at the bottom of the clipboard.

Please don't let it be something big.

"Here you go." He handed her a card stock form. "Keep this on file."

"We're done?"

"Yes. I'm shocked. You had a top-notch project manager. That's for sure. No shortcuts."

"Thank you!" She hugged the inspection sheet. "Thank you so much."

"Good luck. I'm excited to see how things go down here. When I was a kid, this part of the cove was the place to hang out. Your granddad was the coolest guy around."

She walked the inspector to the door and then sat on the floor and cried. *Pops. This is for you.*

CHAPTER SIXTEEN

Elli swept at her tears when she heard the front door open.

"You in here, Elli?"

She really wasn't ready to talk to Brody yet.

"There you are. Hey, what's wrong? Are you crying?" He raced over to where she was still sitting in the floor. "You are. Was the inspector here?"

"Just left," she said, trying to control her voice.

"It can't be that bad. Let me see. We can fix whatever it is. Don't be upset."

"It's not that. We passed."

"We did? That's awesome! Are those happy tears?"

She laughed and then the real sobs just overtook her.

He took her into his arms, and stroked her hair. "What the heck is wrong?"

Elli pulled herself together and moved away from him. He grabbed for her hand and laced their fingers. "You gonna talk to me?"

"I saw Holden this morning."

"Oh?" His expression faded. "You don't still have feelings for him, do you?"

"No." She shook her head.

He looked relieved.

"He told me who you are."

"Elli, you know who I am. We've been working side by side for days. You know me better than anyone. You've snuck your way right into my heart."

"Why didn't you tell me who you really are? I didn't find you by accident on Facebook, did I?"

"I wasn't trying to keep a secret from you."

"But you did."

"It just didn't come up, and in the beginning it was because we were trying to keep things quiet on the second warehouse for R waveStyle to keep it from the competition. So, I'd been watching for any mention of Sand Dollar Cove on social media and I just happen to find your post. It's not like I lied. I had every intention of doing that work for you. It was going to be kind of therapeutic for me. It has been."

"It's not like you needed the work."

"I don't think that was in the job description."

"Well, I thought you were some kind of beach-hopping surfer dude."

"But...I never said that."

"You let me believe it."

"Please don't be mad. I didn't know this was going to turn into...this. And I sure didn't think what I do for a living would bother you so much. I also didn't think in a million years that I was going to meet a girl I'd fall for. I'm crazy about you, Elli."

When he said it she wanted to believe it. So badly, but she didn't want to be hurt again either.

"Look at me." He let go of one of her hands and swept her hair from her face. "I know this sounds crazy, but I'm in love with you. It's fast. I know it. But it feels right. You are an amazing woman."

"You could have anyone."

"I'm well aware of that. And I've never picked any of them. This is different. Wouldn't it be worse if I was pretending to be some successful guy with a profitable company, but was really a beach bum?"

She started laughing. "Yeah. Maybe?"

"I'm sorry. Elli, at first it was just a fun project. But then I started really liking this town, and Nana is amazing. Cooking with her and hanging out was like being with my own grandmother again, and it felt good after losing my dad. It was comforting. And then you...well, that was unexpected."

"What about me?"

"Your spirit. Everything little thing about you. The way you make me feel. I've never felt like this. I like it. A lot. Please don't let this ruin things."

She dried her tears, but her mind was still reeling.

"I can understand you being upset if you've read all that stuff journalists have written about me being the kind of bachelor who will never settle down. And you know, it has been a pretty accurate account up until now. But that's no longer true. I can see myself here. I want to be with you. Don't let Holden try to win you back by making me into something that I'm not."

"He said you were manipulating me so you can hold those surf competitions down here in the cove."

"Elli, if we do that it will be because you and I want that to happen. Trust me, I don't need to steal beach rights for R waveSTYLE. The company has enough money to make a deal pretty much wherever we'd like to. I want you to be a part of all that with me."

"Really? But I'm just a small-town beach girl who loves selling the right house to the right people. You're …"

"In love with you. Please tell me you're feeling it too."

She was afraid to say the words. Instead she tipped her chin and reached up and kissed him.

"I'm going to take that as a yes," he said.

CHAPTER SEVENTEEN

On the Wednesday before Memorial Day weekend, Elli hosted a party for everyone who helped with the rebuilding of the plaza. A huge celebration with whole hogs on smokers and kegs of beer being pumped from giant vats of ice, and Ed was going to perform.

Nana was moved into the Lazy Daisy, and Ed was in the process of making arrangements to move into Sol~Mate.

The festivities were low key, and the weather was perfect for it. A bonfire on the beach lit up the night, and people were talking and laughing. It felt just like the first weekend of the official tourist season should.

Each shop in the plaza was open for a practice run with the locals.

Ever-SOL-Pops was serving up free mini-popsicles. Last year's recipients were there training the kids selected to take over this year, and it looked like they were having a pretty good time.

In the other two kiosks, they'd set up all the utensils for the barbecue and were serving up dinner. Lines were moving quickly, and it appeared the layout was going to really work.

Nana looked like she was queen for a day holding court in the new SandD's Gifts. Brody had hung the sign for her, and it looked brighter and prettier than it ever had on the old building. Her windows were filled with not only her sand dollar art but also art from other North Carolina artisans, which had taken a burden off of her, and she was having so much fun educating everyone on the different pieces.

In the brand new place called Sea Foam they'd be selling beer from a local Carolina brewery on tap and serving tapas. A fun and different place for locals and tourists that planned to be open year round.

R waveSTYLE took the last spot. They were using it to do prototyping on a new line of skimboards, picking up where Elli's granddaddy had left off, renting them by the day to tourists and offering sales of custom boards. They also had outlet prices on overstocks of all of their resort wear. Elli had a feeling the locals might buy out all their stock before they ever got to the weekend.

At seven o'clock Elli had promised announcements and entertainment. Ed had graciously offered to play some acoustic songs, and then a DJ would be pumping out the latest popular music from up in the brand new lifeguard shack R waveSTYLE had sponsored. A donation barrel was set up at the bottom of the guard shack, and people had been dropping in bills all afternoon.

Elli climbed the stairs up to the top of the lifeguard shack. Ed and Brody were already up there.

"You ready?" Brody asked.

"Yep."

Brody flipped on the floodlight. Everyone's attention spun their way. Elli picked up the microphone. "Hey y'all. Can I get your attention?"

Everyone quieted down.

"Thanks. I wanted to first off thank all of you for coming out tonight to celebrate the grand reopening of the plaza."

"Wouldn't have missed it."

"We're here for ya, girl!"

"Whoop."

"Yeah, okay, well I should've known all y'all would show up for barbecue and beer no matter what, but I really do want to thank everyone who helped with the renovations. Can we give a big round of applause for those that gave their time and sweat to the project?"

A loud round of applause, peppered with whistles rose from the beach.

"Nana and I both want to thank you for pulling together to help us rebuild the Shoppes On The Cove. We couldn't have done it without you. Also take note of the boards along the back walls of each shop. Those include the names of all of the original Buy A Board Campaign donors, and all of you who volunteered. I hope everyone will really enjoy the new shops and this end of the beach for the first time in a few decades."

Everyone clapped.

"And a special thank you to our newest resident of Sand Dollar Cove, Ed Rockingham."

"'Freebird'," someone yelled from the crowd.

Ed laughed. "One in every crowd," he teased.

"We realize you moved here for some quiet and anonymity and you really went out of your way to help us. We promise you we will make you glad you chose Sand Dollar Cove for your home."

He raised his longneck beer in the air. "Already am, gal!"

"Now, let's party and start the countdown to opening day!" She cheered, and Brody caught her mid-leap in the air and swung her around.

"Hang on," Ed said. "My buddy here wants to say something before I play."

Elli looked at Ed and shrugged. Maybe he expected a more formal introduction. Did he mean her? She'd made all the announcements she'd planned to.

Brody took the microphone from Ed. "Thanks. I have something to add."

"What are you doing?" Elli whispered.

"I also wanted to share that R waveSTYLE has reallocated some of our marketing fund to host an annual skimboarding competition here on the beach, and Elli has been helping me with the details. Marketing will go gangbusters tomorrow worldwide for the end of July event."

Everyone cheered, and Elli hugged his neck and he pressed a kiss to hers.

He turned his attention back to the people at the gathering. "When I decided to set up an East Coast operation for R waveSTYLE, I had no idea just what a great location I'd found. Not only is it perfectly located along the Eastern Seaboard, and on one of the nicest beaches around, but the people here are exactly the kind of people I want to work for us. And exactly the kind of people I want to spend my time with." He turned to Elli. "Especially you, Elli Eversol."

He reached for her hand.

"I figure if we can rebuild a building in just a few days, meeting my future wife in just the course of a couple months is about the accurate speed calculation for how fast things can happen in here in Sand Dollar Cove."

Someone wolf-whistled from the crowd.

"Elli, if you'd do me the honor, you'd make this surf bum the happiest wave rider around." He took to one knee. "Will you be my bride? Because the first day I showed up at the Sol~Mate, I met my soul mate, and I don't want to spend a single day without you by my side."

Her legs went weak. Thank goodness he was holding her hand, because otherwise she might topple right over. She grabbed his arm with her other hand. "Yes! Yes, I'll marry you."

Brody handed the microphone back to Ed, then gathered her into his arms.

It didn't even matter that hundreds of people looked on as he kissed her, because nothing but Brody mattered at this moment. Her heart was so full she could barely breathe. "I love you," she said.

"2020."

His sweet mention of the loving tradition her grandparents had shared made joyful tears tickle her lashes. Every moment her love seemed to deepen for him.

Ed put the microphone in the stand and played a few chords to one of Cal's most popular songs. "I'll host the wedding right here. How about it? Beachfront wedding?" Ed said.

The crowd cheered, but the noise seemed to fall away. She looked into Brody's eyes. "Can we? Would you be okay with that?"

He moved closer, his breath fanning her face. "Whatever you want. Just don't make me wait too long to start our forever."

"It's already begun."

Acknowledgements

This story was written for and first exclusively available in the SWEET TALK box set to raise money to find the cure for diabetes. Thank you to Brenda Novak who has raised hundreds of thousands of dollars for the cause and for letting me be a part that body of work.

Heartfelt appreciation to Deb Nemeth and Tom Justice for making this story sparkle with their editing talents.

To Chrystal Yates for answering my real estate questions and helping me make my way from Virginia born-and-raised to Carolina girl as I settled into my new home here in North Carolina.

A special shout-out to my Aunt Ru and Uncle Sonny for the wonderful memories made those summers on the Carolina shore.

Thank you, to my family and friends, for always being there for me. I'm blessed to be surrounded by wonderful people who make my life so complete. Love y'all!

AND TO ALL OF YOU READING THIS ~ THANK YOU!

About the Author

Nancy Naigle writes love stories from the crossroad of small town and suspense.

Born and raised in Virginia Beach, Nancy now calls North Carolina home.

Stay in touch with Nancy on Facebook, twitter or subscribe to her newsletter on her website.

Read. Relax. Repeat.
www.NancyNaigle.com